MIRACLE OF THE ROSE

by Ramnath Subramanian

For my wife, Maria Subramanian,
editor par excellence,
who is the love of my life,
and the source of my daily inspiration

Word had gotten around that Gopal was starting school. So, when he emerged from his house accompanied by his grandmother, Linda, and Raman, a small group of people was waiting outside to cheer him on. Along the way, they encountered more people who had come out to show their support.

The grandmother was quite overwhelmed. "I never thought all these people were going to show up for my boy," she said.

Gopal had his blue backpack on and a tiffin carrier in his hand,—both items purchased for him by Linda,—and walked proudly. A man about to climb a mountain or go on a momentous sea voyage could not have stretched out his stride in a more purposeful fashion.

"This is quite a treat," said Linda. "I could almost cry."

Raman had his camera and tripod with him and recorded Gopal's journey in documentary style.

The principal was waiting for them outside the school's gate with some of his staff, as was a group of reporters and photographers. Anjali Dutt of the Daily Beacon was there and procured the first interview.

"What are your thoughts about school?" she asked.

Gopal didn't hear the question because his mind had run away to Praarthana Hill. "The holy man is no longer there," he told himself, allowing a touch of sadness to enter his mind. "He said he would be back, but he didn't say when."

The reporter repeated the question, and this time Gopal answered. "I'm very excited about going to school," he said. "I want to learn English, so I can talk to memsahib without someone translating everything for me. Also, I want to improve my Hindi so I can have clever conversations with the holy man."

"How come the holy man is not here to send you off to school?" asked another reporter, encroaching on the interview in progress.

Linda sensed that Gopal was nonplussed by the question, and came to his aid.

"The holy man is everywhere," she said.

"I don't see him," returned the reporter, in a somewhat sarcastic tone.

A woman Linda recalled seeing on the day of the second miracle on Praarthana Hill was standing next to them. She did not care for the sarcasm at all, and said, "That's because you're looking with your eyes,—you need to see with your heart."

No further escalation of this topic happened because the principal gathered the school staff together for a group photograph. Then he read from a prepared statement:

Thank you all for coming to this special event. It was not such a long time ago that the holy man moved into the burned-out house on Praarthana Hill. The two miracles he performed there are still fresh in our minds.

The special attachment our new student Gopal formed with the holy man and the unique role he played in those two miracles have made him a byword in every household in Mala Nagar, and beyond.

Today will be Gopal's first day in school ever, and as you can imagine he has some catching up to do,—but he is a smart young boy and will do fine. I'm sure God will see him through any difficulties he faces along the way.

Now, I'll ask Gopal to say a few words.

Linda gave him a nod of encouragement. Raman, who was standing to the side recording the event, looked up from the camera and gave him a thumbs-up.

An explosion of flashbulbs went off as Gopal came forward. "If I'm going to school today, it's because of Memsahib Linda,—and the holy man, of course," said Gopal. "The holy man told me that one day I'll be building a palace on Praarthana Hill,—right where the burned-out house sits now. You can't build a palace without going to school, can you?

"I also want you to write in your stories that I'm the best gilli danda player in Mala Nagar. Before I build a palace on the hill, I'm going to become the gilli danda champion of the world."

With that Gopal came forward, gave Linda a big hug, waved to Raman, and started walking towards the school. Anjali caught up to him and concluded her interview with a few more questions.

The first bell sounded for students to get to the assembly hall. After the second bell, which announced that school was in session, Linda and Raman made their way to the Ganesh Tea Stall.

The Ganesh Tea Stall was a modest establishment close to Linda's apartment on Main Street. It offered seating under a thatched roof that was supported by four bamboo poles, and was frequented by the locals who came there to enjoy a cup of chai and talk about cricket, politics, and local gossip.

The owner was a man with a stern voice and brusque manners, but his patrons liked him in spite of these qualities because he was always forthright with his opinions. If he had a name, no one knew it, and it was rumored that he had a past that was well worth hiding.

He offered an offhanded greeting, and said, "So what's new?"

"Gopal's in school," said Linda. She wanted to affect a matter-of-fact attitude, but her pride showed through nonetheless.

"That truly is a miracle," said the owner. "I never thought I'd live to see the day when Gopal went to school."

Just a month or so ago, Gopal was running around the streets causing mischief, and his attitude— cheeky and sometimes disrespectful— was abhorred by the shopkeepers, especially the owner of the tea stall.

"Gopal is a changed boy, that's for sure," conceded the owner.

"Thanks in large part to Linda," said Raman.

"Well, things are going to be a little bit different going forward," said Linda, "because the holy man has gone away,—that's according to Gopal."

The owner was not a man easily shocked by events, but he stopped what he was doing and looked at them in disbelief.

"Where has he gone to?" he asked.

"We don't know. He told Gopal it was temporary."

"You can't trust people,—makes no difference if they are holy or not," said the owner, in a voice packed with cynicism. "As I said before, holy men come and go. The town needs a break from all this talk about miracles. We need to get back to normal."

Raman didn't agree with this sentiment at all. "He brought people hope and a sense of rejuvenation," he said. "They'll miss him for sure on the hill."

A sudden influx of customers took the owner back behind the counter to prepare some snacks and to brew another pot of chai.

Linda took out a magazine from her purse and gave it to Raman. "The holy man sent this to me. He earmarked a page,—take a look at it."

Raman turned the magazine to the earmarked page and gaped at it.

"How did he know you were interested in the Kumortuli Potters' Colony?"

"How did he know to send me the page that advertised your talk at the college?" returned Linda. "Without that, the chances are we wouldn't have met." She paused, and then added, "Truth is, he knows a lot of things without knowing about them. How he does that, I don't know. I guess that's why he's a holy man."

"So, are you going to Kumortuli?"

"I have to, don't you think?"

"I do," said Raman, with a smile. "I also think I should go along with you. I've been to Calcutta before, and I can be your guide. It also fits in with my plan because I want to make a documentary about the famous flower market, which is right next to the potters' colony."

Linda thought for a while. "We should wait for a week or two,—allow Gopal to get settled in at school. We'll also need someone to look after him,—walk him to school, help him with his school work, and so on. Maybe Ravi will take care of it. I know he's moving to Bijli, but that's not for another two months. I think he'll do it."

ii

Gopal came out of school at two o'clock. Linda and Raman were waiting for him at the main gate. He came running towards them,— ebullient, full of positive energy, and most eager to show them all the work he had done.

He impressed Linda with a few short English sentences, relying for variety on three-letter nouns and prepositions. "A cat is on a box," he said, absolutely delighted with himself. Linda and Raman clapped their hands and made over the exhibition.

Gopal wanted to see if the old man had left a message for him. The day was slightly overcast and the temperature was agreeable, so they decided to take a leisurely walk to Praarthana Hill.

The people, having no knowledge of the holy man's departure, were pullulating the landscape with their presence. A long line stretched from the base of the hill to the house along a zigzag path. The two policemen managing the crowd knew about Gopal's special status and let him move ahead of the line.

Before the miracles happened, Gopal used to sneak past the policemen and enter the house through a window in the back. Today, he walked straight in, while Linda and Raman waited outside.

Two singers, a violinist, and a mridangam player were setting up their positions on a wooden platform that had been erected next to a peepul tree in front of the house.

"I'm glad to see the boy," said an old woman, who was waiting by the steps leading to the front door. "He may bring us some news from the holy man."

Gopal entered the room. As expected, the holy man was not there. The mat that used to be on the floor was gone, as also the duffel bag that contained his meager belongings. Gopal looked around the room to see if there was a message left anywhere. Yes, there it was,—a piece of paper lying on the floor next to the window, weighted down with a small pebble. Gopal ran towards it and picked it up. The holy man had written notes before to Linda, and Gopal had acted as the carrier for these messages. This, though, was the first note that was written to him.

Gopal,

I'm glad you had a good first day at school. I was very proud to see you standing there, smartly dressed, ready for school. I watched from a distance, leaning against a tree,—you would not have noticed me.

Keep working hard at school. Make every subject you're studying into a gilli danda, and come out on top as the champion.

Don't forget to visit the river from time to time. And if you should run into the homeless man with a white beard,—who you think is me in disguise,—say hello to him.

I expect that when I come back to Praarthana Hill,—I don't know when,—you and I will talk to each other a little bit in English.

Stay straight as an arrow with your goals, and pure as the songs in the Poornima River.

The note was signed off with the holy symbol "Om." In the right bottom corner was a small sketch of a cat sitting on a box.

Gopal couldn't believe his eyes. How did the holy man know about that?

He came running out of the house, clutching the note in his hand. Memsahib was right: the holy man was everywhere, and he knew everything.

People watched Gopal's animation, and they heard the excitement in his voice.

"What did the holy man say to you?" asked the woman, who was standing next to the steps.

"The holy man has gone away and won't be back for a while," is what he would have told the woman before seeing the note, but now his perspective had become altered.

A crowd of people was pushing forward, eager to hear what the boy had to say.

"Step back!" shouted a policeman, afraid that people would trample on each other.

"He said to keep on praying and to keep on singing," Gopal said, and taking the pebble out of his pocket, gave it to the woman.

"Jeete raho, beta," she said, her voice shaking with gratitude. "Jeete raho."

iii

Before going to bed, Linda sat down at the kitchen table and contemplated her life. She had given a nod to going on a trip to Kumortuli with Raman. Was she being reckless? Of course she was,—two failed marriages, neither of which had lasted more than two years, should have proved to her that she was a terrible judge of men. So, why was she walking into a potential new entanglement?

She was fond of Raman,—she liked his friendly disposition, his unassuming attitude, and the fire that came into his eyes when he talked passionately about subjects dear to his heart,—but it was all within the purview of friendship.

"There's no need to be on guard, to be cautionary," she told herself.

Somehow that didn't sound convincing to her, especially when she considered his emotional reaction to her thoughts on returning to London.

"You can't go back to London!" he had protested. "You are a fixture of Mala Nagar. Besides, who'll take care of Gopal's schooling?"

She had decided to stay on, of course,—independent of his opinion,—but that early exchange hinted at something slightly more than an equation in the calculus of friendship.

She went to the window, opened the shutters, and looked outside. One floor below was a general store that sold a variety of food items used for cooking. Even though it was past eight, people were still shopping. Main Street, which ran all the way to Praarthana Hill in one direction and to the riverbank in the opposite direction, was busy as usual, and the blaring horns and clanging bells from cars, lorries, rickshaws, and carts announced the sanguine nature of business even at this late hour.

"This is India," Linda told herself. "I have to forget the map of London, my footsteps there, and start afresh. I have to erase the shadows from my past, because the new geography demands it."

She went to the writing table, sat down, and took out from its drawer the notes that the holy man had sent her. As she read them again, the image of the Poornima River arose in her mind,—it was central to the holy man's existence and his thinking.

The second note read:

If someone offers you a leaf, a flower, a fruit, or water, accept it,—for the conversations in the river have touched all these objects and sanctified them. They are all infused with the miracle of life.

"That is the approach to take," she told herself. "Kumortuli is an offering,—take it. See how the river's chatter is in that part of the country, and embrace the songs that it brings to your life. The biggest mistake is to walk around afraid that you will make a mistake."

Having reached this resolve, Linda went back to the window, looked outside, and breathed in the air. It filled her mind with a new strength and a feeling of wellbeing.

It was after her second divorce that she flung herself into the pursuit of a master's degree in anthropology, and the research topic she picked—Potters and Image Makers of India—had brought her to Mala Nagar. Her original intent was to stay for two months, but that had become rearranged since the holy man and Gopal entered the circle of her life.

"The river has a way of taking you to places that were not configured in your plans," she said to herself. "The trick is to flow with the current,—recognizing that, ultimately, you're not in charge; that destiny has a role to play in all the chapters."

She thought about the apartment she had shared with her friend Madeline near Putney Bridge in London. That picture seemed a million miles away, in a different galaxy.

All her belongings were still in the apartment. She would have to ask Maddy to put them in storage for her. As for her degree, she would have to postpone classes for a semester or two, or abandon the whole project completely. She had no idea what she was going to do, and it didn't seem to matter too much to her anymore.

It was just two months ago that she was taking a leisurely walk along the River Thames, shopping at Harrods, and looking at the paintings of Titian and Constable at the National Gallery. Funny how things can assume a great distance when the mind wanders into a new reality.

The holy man appeared to have got rid of all distinctions in all matters. For him, the River Thames, the Poornima River, and all other rivers were synonymous. "Here" and "there" carried the same meaning, and he could be in both places at once. She wondered if he had achieved these cognitive skills and physical abilities with meditation. But how does he get the power to perform miracles?

Some questions have no answers, and this was one of them.

The first miracle happened after Gopal informed the townspeople that something special was going to happen on the forthcoming Friday. There was no way to confirm this since the holy man spoke to no one, except Gopal. The news brought hundreds to the house on Praarthana Hill. Gopal had spread the rumor just to create drama, but the holy man now felt the need to do something for the people who had gathered at the house. On Friday, he and Gopal watered a nearly lifeless rosebush that was sitting in a flower pot in front of the house. The scraggly bush that had suffered both the fire and months of neglect, and didn't have a single green leaf or bud, suddenly sprang to life.

The second miracle revived a young girl from a long coma.

As Linda remembered these events, a feeling of awe and joy passed through her like a bolt of electricity. While people in Piccadilly Circus and Trafalgar Square were going about their lives in the midst of grandeur and luxury,—pretty fountains, imposing buildings, and all the rest,—here she was in Mala Nagar witnessing miracles, and actually being a part of the miracles because of her connection to Gopal.

She suddenly felt rich and blessed to be in Mala Nagar. She wondered what life was going to bring her in the coming months. She also looked forward to the holy man returning to the burned-out house. His presence there gave her and all the people comfort and a feeling of security.

The store below was getting ready to close. The traffic on Main Street had thinned by a slight margin. She pictured the house on the hill,—all the people filing past it; all the people camping in the enclosure created by the police, waiting for the holy man to make an appearance, waiting for another miracle. Faith is a wonderful thing, she thought—it defies all known limitations and reaches towards the impossible and the miraculous.

Tomorrow she was meeting Raman for lunch. She looked forward to that very much. The morning, though, would start with a walk to the school, with Gopal at her side. Raman had said he would join her.

Gopal's second day in school,—what new things would he be learning? By what length would his English improve beyond "A cat is on a box?"

He's like the river himself, she thought,—full of lilt, energy, and warmth. That's why the holy man speaks to him, has a special bond with him.

Linda took another look at the street below, and then closed the shutters. She looked forward to sleep and to another day in Mala Nagar.

iv

Ashoka Restaurant was crowded for the lunch hour and there was no table to be had.

"Come in, come in," said the owner, showing great solicitude. "As you can see, we're full, but I can put a folding table in the back if that's all right with you."

"No need to trouble yourself,— we'll wait," said Raman, and Linda echoed that sentiment.

The owner lowered his voice to a conspiratorial whisper, and said, "There's a rumor floating around that the holy man is no longer staying at the house. Is that true?"

"As you know, the holy man is in and out of the house constantly,—although no one sees him leaving or coming back," said Raman, evasively. "We'll have your lunch special and chai."

"Very good, sir," said the owner.

They had to wait ten minutes to be seated, but the food was served right away.

No sooner were the plates in front of them than a middle-aged woman approached them. "You will pardon me for interrupting," she said, "but I have a small favor to ask of you. If it is possible, will you ask Gopal to take a small item to the holy man so it can receive his blessing? It will mean a lot to my sister who is very ill."

Linda thought it was an opportune moment to tell the truth. "The holy man is not at the house, and he won't be there for a while."

The woman was incredulous. "Are you sure about this?"

"I cannot be sure," said Linda, in a sympathetic voice. "I'm going by what Gopal told me. He usually gets his stories straight."

"It's all my fault. I should have gone to the hill when my sister asked me to, and I'd have seen him for sure."

Linda tried to comfort her by saying that the holy man would be back, but her distress was such that immediate amelioration was not possible.

"I must speak to Gopal," said the woman, in a voice filled with agitation. "I need to find out when the holy man will be coming back. The boy talks to the holy man,—he's bound to know."

"He doesn't know anything more than what I've told you," said Linda. "What item is it that you want the holy man to bless?"

"It's a necklace. My sister has worn it ever since she was a little girl. When she was at the temple in Guruvayoor, the priest there said a special prayer and blessed it. She believes it has special powers to protect her. The holy man's blessing will make it extra special." The woman paused, and Linda could tell by looking at her face that a new strand of thought had entered her mind. "How come all the people are still on the hill?" she asked.

Linda shrugged her shoulders. "Even if they know he has gone away, they may be waiting for him to come back. He never really goes away, though, because his spirit is always there in the house."

She recalled every word of the last message the holy man had sent her:

The river that runs between your house and my house is calling me to a new destination, temporarily. I told Gopal that I will return; and I will. In the meantime, let him know that when I am there, I'm still here. There is no such thing as distance where the heart rules.
Om

She suddenly remembered that she had a vial of the river water blessed by the holy man in her purse. She brought it out and gave it to the woman.

"Oh, you're an angel sent down by the gods!" said the woman, overcome with gratitude. With a profusion of thanks, and saying "namaste" a few times to show her reluctance for saying goodbye, she withdrew, and went back to her table.

"When we are in Kumortuli, we can enjoy lunch without interruptions," said Raman.

"Oh, I don't mind the interruptions," returned Linda. "Sometimes, an interruption turns out to be better than the main event, just as a detour may become more profitable than the final destination."

"I like your perspective," said Raman, showing admiration, "and that gleam that comes into your eyes when you're engaged in mischief,—cerebral mischief, in this case. I bet you were a good debater at school."

"My mother would disagree with you,—she often accused me of being scatterbrained."

This was the first time she had mentioned her family, and she wondered if Raman would express his curiosity in some way. He did not.

"My father, on the other hand, considered that I was made of solid stuff. Funny how two people so close to me had such divergent opinions."

Raman gave a wry smile. "Both my parents think of me as a disappointment," he said. "Do you want to know why?"

"I can't imagine."

"They expected me to marry a nice girl in a well-arranged marriage and give them lots of grandchildren. They love me all the same, but I think it irks them that I'm still a bachelor."

The door was open for Linda. This was the best opportunity for her to unburden herself. "You're not doing as bad as me," she said. "I'm twice divorced. You'll find a lot of divorced women in London, but only a few, I'm sure, who are twice divorced. The good news is I had very little to do with those two disasters. If I'm guilty of anything, it's that I'm a bad judge of character."

Raman received the news with kind equanimity. "We are none of us to blame," he said. "Marriage is a funny thing. It either works out or it doesn't, regardless of anticipation, expectation, exploration, and commitment. If God smiles on a marriage, it will succeed. I believe that divinity is a part of all good things."

Then they talked about their trip,—possible dates, train schedule, places to see in Calcutta,—and Linda soon felt an excitement building up inside her,—an excitement akin to what she had felt when she got on the plane headed to India.

v

Linda was not a stranger to train travel in India,—she had taken a train to get to Mala Nagar. That said, she still found the experience fascinating, especially for the resiliency shown by Indian travelers to endure a long journey without all the comforts that a Londoner like herself would consider customary.

She and Raman occupied two window seats on one side of the aisle in a third-class sleeper, while six others were seated on the other side. At night, the backs of their seats would be brought down to create the lower berth, where Linda planned to sleep.

A father and a mother with their two boys and two men sat across from them. The boys were playing some kind of a paper-and-pencil game, the mother was knitting what looked like a sweater, and the father appeared content to be doing nothing. Of the two men, one was reading a newspaper, while the other was getting some snacks out of a white cloth bag.

Outside, rice fields, groves, huts, and dirt paths flashed past the window. Children standing next to the railroad tracks, with bare feet and tattered clothing, waved to the passing train.

"I've always enjoyed train rides," said Raman. "As a youngster, I would stretch my hand outside the window to feel the sting from the hot coal particles streaming past the window. What I liked best was when the train stopped at a station that was teeming with activity and bursting with energy, as people looking for their names on the cars, coolies walking at great speed with unimaginable loads on their turbaned heads, and people selling all kinds of things, created great drama."

"For me," said Linda, "a train journey in England was so efficient and orderly that there was no adventure in it whatsoever. You looked out the window to pass the time, and then got to your destination,—maybe you read part of a book along the way. No ticketless traveler ever played hide-and-seek with the conductor, and no one hopped on to the train as it approached the station to sell toys, trinkets, and food items. All these scenes in India fascinate me no end."

The man sitting across the aisle from Linda lowered his newspaper to reveal a bearded, spectacled face that was very serious in its countenance.

"Westerners collect these impressions and then go home and write a book or make a movie. In the meantime the struggle goes on for the people to earn a living wage."

The comment was offered casually, but it packed a jab of criticism.

"I'm sure there is some truth in what you say," said Linda.

"There's a lot of truth in what I say," returned the man. "The British Raj mentality still exists and it wants to show India wearing wretched clothes. Forget the music, forget the dance, forget the dignity of the hardworking man, and show instead, endless footage of the slums of Calcutta, and people bathing in the river by the Howrah Bridge."

"Aren't you painting with a very broad brush?" asked Raman.

"Am I? The British notion of India being a Third World country is palpably real. What the media do is soften it by throwing in some mysticism, or pointing to the peculiar charm of a god who has an elephant's head or a goddess who has eight arms. India is often painted as a caricature of a nation."

Linda was listening to the man with great interest. The other passengers, including the children, were entirely oblivious to his harangue.

"It is interesting that you bring up mysticism," said Linda, "because I think Indian mysticism is a powerful force. We have a holy man living in Mala Nagar who has changed the geography of the town,—both literally and metaphorically. He is no caricature,—he has performed two miracles."

"I read about it in the papers," interjected the man. "Is it true what they say in the papers?"

"I don't know what they said about him in the papers, but Raman and I witnessed the miracles, as did many other people. I can tell you this,—world politics becomes a rather small and insignificant item when you consider what is happening in Mala Nagar."

"My name is Rishi Sharma," said the man. The hard lines on his face had softened suddenly, and he gave them a friendly smile. Linda and Raman introduced themselves.

"I must visit Mala Nagar and meet this holy man," said Rishi. "By the way, where are you staying in Calcutta?"

"We were thinking about finding a hotel on Park Street."

"Think no more. I have a large house in the Tollygunge area. I invite you to be my guests. I will not take no for an answer."

The suddenness and largesse of the offer and the intensity with which it was made surprised Linda.

"I don't know what to say."

"Don't say anything," said Rishi. "I'll be honored. I must introduce myself more fully. I am the president of Wheels of India Foundation. I sponsor projects that celebrate India. I'm married and I have three children, two of whom are living at home."

When Rishi found out the nature and scope of the work that Linda and Raman were currently engaged in, his enthusiasm climbed another notch.

"You and I need to have a long talk about your documentaries," he said to Raman. Then turning to Linda, he added, "I must arrange a meeting between you and Aruna Roy,—she's considered an expert in the field of pottery and handicrafts. She is not in the city right now, but I must arrange a meeting for a later time. I think you will find the connection valuable."

Linda took out the holy man's second note from her purse and handed it to Rishi.

"We accept your offer in the spirit of the holy man's message," she said.

Linda then explained the situation in Mala Nagar in greater details. Rishi was surprised when he found out that Linda and the holy man had never spoken to each other. "Yet he has written you notes that point to a very meaningful association," he said. He was also enamored of the Gopal story.

When the train finally reached Howrah Station, Linda, Raman, and Rishi were conversing like old friends.

"If you're wondering why I'm traveling third class, it's because of what my father told me a number of times. He said that I should walk in the shoes of the average man now and then so I don't lose track of what life is really about. Besides, without traveling third class, I wouldn't have met the two of you,—so there's that."

As the train came to a stop, he added, "I hope my driver Ramnaresh has got the date and time of our train right. He's a very nice man,—I've had him in my service for 20 years,—but I cannot honesty say that he is reliable. Last time when I arrived by train from Shantiniketan, I had to hire a taxi to get home. He's quite a character,—you'll like him."

vi

Rishi's house was a mansion which was reached by a long, curving, gravel driveway lined with trees. The front of it was semicircular, and three robust columns supported a balcony on the second floor.

As soon as the car pulled up to the front, the large wooden doors swung open and a woman came running out.

"I'm glad you're back," she said, flailing her arms and looking quite flustered. "Everything is in a mess."

"What's in a mess?" asked Rishi, getting out of the car, as Ramnaresh helped to take out the luggage and bring it to the doorstep.

"You're not listening to me,—everything!" she repeated.

"Surely, some things are still working," said Rishi, exhibiting stellar equanimity.

"Well, the water pressure has dropped,—so there is hardly any water coming out of the taps. The cook has taken ill, and something happened at college with Lalitha,—she says she won't be going back."

"My wife, Savitri," said Rishi. Then turning to his wife, "These are two new friends of mine. I met them on the train,—Linda and Raman. They'll be staying with us for a few days. I'll have Ramnaresh get hold of the maintenance man. As for the cook being disabled by illness, we'll have to hire a temporary cook or do some work in the kitchen ourselves. And if I have to guess, Lali is just going through another dramatic phase in her life."

As they entered the house, Savitri turned to her guests for sympathy. "My husband is the kind of man who would be conducting an orchestra while the Titanic is sinking. Whoever said patience is a virtue got it all wrong. By the way, it's a pleasure to meet you both and have you as our guests."

The foyer was elegantly decorated with carpeting, chandelier, and paintings. Directly in front of the door, an L-shaped staircase offered access to the second floor.

As they went up the stairs, Savitri seemed still upset by the calamities of the day.

"I can't believe we have guests and they're going to starve," she said, with masterful exaggeration.

"No one is going to starve," said Rishi. "We will take them out to lunch."

"Finally, you've said something sensible," said his wife. Then turning to Linda, she added, "We'll let you have the two rooms at the end of the hall. The guest room is slightly larger than the other, which belonged to my son when he was living with us. Now he is at IIT Kharagpur, pursuing a degree in electrical engineering." Linda noticed that when she talked about her son, pride shone in her eyes.

After freshening up, they were ready to leave, but Ramnaresh had gone in search of the maintenance man without telling anyone,—so they had to wait for his return. This delay, however, proved useful, because they used the time to exchange stories and anecdotes while sitting in the living room. Savitri got to know everything there was to know about the happenings in Mala Nagar, and she was fascinated by the special connection that the holy man had forged with Gopal.

"I think holiness and innocence go hand in hand," said Raman. "Children have no designs,— their conversations are natural. I think the holy man is able to talk to Gopal in that natural way,— like the flow of a river, to use his favorite metaphor."

"You are absolutely right," said Savitri. "Have you noticed that holy men don't show up in big cities, but rather in small towns like Mala Nagar,—why is that?" The question was rhetorical. "It is because God wants us to move away from the melee and corruption of big cities to smaller towns and villages."

"That is stretching it a little bit," said her husband, "although I do believe it is easier to find God in a rice field than in a factory."

"We must visit Mala Nagar very soon," said Savitri, in a voice charged with resolution, but then turning to Linda, added, "but you say the holy man has gone away."

"He promised to come back, but he didn't say when."

The conversation then turned to the purpose of their visit, and it was decided that Ramnaresh would drop them off in the morning at their first destination and pick them up from the location that was last on their day's itinerary.

"But first," said Rishi, "I'm going to use tomorrow to show you all the sights of Calcutta."

At this juncture, Ramnaresh's voice was heard outside, and four hungry people filed out of the house to tackle lunch at Vivek's Kitchen.

vii

Linda and Raman felt completely at home in the Tollygunge mansion. The incessant banter between Rishi and Savitri, combined with their proclivity to take opposite sides on any issue and argue their points soulfully, created an atmosphere where the visitors felt that they could let their guards down. This play of opposites became manifest at Vivek's Kitchen as husband and wife debated the merits and shortcomings of various dishes. Being astute, the waiter made a second appearance to make sure that the order he had written down on his notepad agreed with what the Sharmas really wanted.

"I'm glad you checked back," said Savitri to the waiter. "I'm sorry, but I was not able to convince my husband to change his order to a better choice. He's a hardheaded man, and there's nothing I can do about it."

"I'm not hardheaded,—I just like to eat what I please," protested Rishi, with a smile.

The gentle ribbing continued until the food was served, at which point a uniform harmony descended upon the table. Everyone praised the food and the service. Rishi effused about the macher jhol, and Savitri, taking a spoonful from his plate and tasting it, concurred with her husband's opinion. Raman said that if he was more informed on the culinary front, he would be tempted to create a documentary about Calcutta's cuisine. The meal ended with rasgullas, sandesh, and coffee.

After the meal, they decided to take a walk along Dhakuria Lake.

"You know a lot about trees," said Linda, as Savitri pointed out the kanak champa tree and talked about the fragrant blooms it sported in March.

When they got to the peepul tree, Raman said, "I know this tree,—there's one in front of the house on Prayer Hill."

"Yes, it's a sacred tree," said Savitri. "In the Bhagavad Gita, Lord Krishna says that he is the peepul among the trees. Also, Buddha attained enlightenment while meditating under a peepul tree."

When they got back to the house, Ramnaresh added another layer to the drama by injecting himself into their company to make an oblique and inconsequential comment.

Savitri was talking to Linda about bokul flowers when Ramnaresh came into the room and made the announcement that it was not going to rain.

"Who said it is going to rain?" asked Savitri, showing a mix of exasperation and puzzlement.

"I can feel it in my bones when it's going to rain. I thought you should know,—that way you can make full plans for the day."

"Rain or no rain, we're going ahead with full plans," interjected Rishi.

Savitri regarded her husband with eyes filled with playful reproach. "It's a moot point, dear. Ramnaresh has already told us that it's not going to rain."

"Even if it was going to rain," continued Rishi, but Savitri let the topic drop and returned to talking about bokul.

"You should wear flowers in your hair," she said. "I think it will make you look very pretty."

Raman resolved right then that when they visited the flower market he was going to buy a string of jasmine for Linda's hair.

That evening, after doing some shopping and attending a lecture at the Ramakrishna Mission titled "The Unseen in Religion," Linda and Raman spent some time in a small garden that was in the back of the house. They looked forward to the city tour the following day, and Linda was reading a few paragraphs from the guide book she had picked up in the library, when she noticed that Raman was distracted with a faraway look in his eyes.

Indeed, Raman was distracted. He was thinking about the perfect symmetry of Linda's nose and mouth, and how the golden tresses framed her face to great advantage. He imagined her with a strand of jasmine adorning her hair. Should it go on the right side or the left?

"Are you listening?" asked Linda, her voice chiming in like temple bells in a pastoral setting.

"Yes, yes," said Raman, breaking away from the vision. "I was listening to every word you said. You were reading about the Victoria Memorial."

She was right,—his mind had wandered off,—but she didn't challenge his assertion, didn't point out that she had moved past Victoria Memorial and was reading about the Writers' Building. She simply smiled and continued reading.

viii

Ramnaresh prognosticated about the weather prior to their departure and gave it the green light. His bones did not detect any mischief-making in the meteorological aspects of the day.

They drove along Chowringhee Raod and made their first stop at the Victoria Memorial. This was followed by a visit to St. Paul's Cathedral. Linda took in the historical details, but she was not drawn to either of these two structures,—they reminded her too much of London, and Europe in general. The Maidan, likewise, gave comfort, as all stretches of green space do in a city, but there was nothing unique about it.

The next stop, though, took her breath away. She had never seen anything like it before,—a long stretch of street, maybe half a mile long, packed tightly with stores selling nothing but books, and lots of them. Books were piled from floor to ceiling, and columns of books also occupied the front of the stores. Shelves had been placed against tree trunks to display additional hardbacks. The street was a sea of books and hundreds of people were actively engaged in perusing and purchasing them,—many trading books or haggling over the price.

"People in England and America make a lot of the reading habit, but I bet they haven't seen anything like this. What's amazing is, ask any of these shopkeepers for an obscure title,—it could be in French, German, or Russian,—and he will have it in your hands in a minute or two."

Just as Rishi made this comment, Linda watched a man go by,—he was carrying a bundle of books secured with a string in each of his hands, while another bundle was perched on his head. The fact that he walked at a brisk pace to add to some shopkeeper's inventory was proof that book business was brisk business in the colony of books known as Boi Para.

Raman was talking to Linda about the literacy rate in West Bengal and comparing it to that of other states in India, when a teenage girl engaged them in conversation.

"I show madam best bookshop in College Street,—three books for 50 rupees. My father's shop, —best in College Street."

"What kind of books do you sell?" asked Linda.

"All kind of books, madam,—very good books, high quality, very cheap."

Linda looked closely at the girl. She wore a long skirt of pastel colors and her long-sleeve blouse was teal with green borders. She wore a thin necklace and the gloss of her braided, jet hair played with the sunbeams.

"Do you have any books on Kumortuli?" asked Linda.

"Yes, we do."

"And the flower market?" chimed in Raman.

"Yes, sir."

"Here's 50 rupees for those books, and you may add one on potteries. Also, keep this twenty for yourself."

"Thank you, madam. Thank you very much."

The girl received the money and took off on the run.

"If she doesn't come back, you've lost 70 rupees," said Rishi.

"Oh, she'll come back. I studied her face,—she has honest eyes."

Linda's assessment proved accurate: the girl was back within 20 minutes.

She came running towards them, and handing the books to Linda, said, "I hope madam likes these books. The book about Kumortuli,—the writer is my dad's friend. It has many pictures."

The books' titles—*The Magic of Kumortuli*, *The Flower Market of Calcutta*, and *The Potters of Midnapore*—showed that the young girl had fulfilled her obligation to a T.

"Perfect," said Linda, giving the girl a nice smile. "Thank you so much."

The girl lingered a little and walked alongside them. "My father happy that I make business for him," she said.

"I hope you sell lots of books today," said Raman.

"I hope so too," said Linda, and gave her another smile.

The girl took a few more steps, then fell back, and soon was lost among the crowd.

"Makes me think of Gopal,—" said Raman. "a girl version of him, except that she has a father, and possibly a mother as well."

Linda felt a little homesick for Mala Nagar. She wondered how Gopal was getting along with school, and if he had gotten another message from the holy man.

She was leafing through the Kumortuli book while listening to Raman and Rishi, when she stopped dead in her tracks. "Look at this!" she exclaimed.

She gave the index card that was inside the book to Raman. Rishi leaned over to take a look at it. It read:

One door opens another door.
Om

"It's in the holy man's handwriting!" she said. She reached into her purse and produced the message that the holy man had written her. "Look at the writing,—the resemblance is striking."

"It looks very much like his handwriting," agreed Rishi.

"How did that get in the book, and what does it mean?" asked Raman.

Linda had felt a faint connection to the girl, and it seemed that the holy man wanted her to press on with it,—but how was she to do that when she didn't know her name or the name of her father's business? She flipped through the pages of the books to see if anything else was tucked inside them. Drawing a blank, she looked in the back of the books to see if there was any sticker or rubber stamp advertising the business. There was none.

"But what if I do know where to find the girl,—what then?" she asked herself. "I have to wait until I have some clarity in the matter. It will come, surely, but when or in what form, I do not know."

Raman and Rishi were still talking about the note when Linda rejoined the conversation.

"If it is indeed a note written by the holy man, it's a most extraordinary thing,—a mini-miracle," said Rishi, "and you are at the center of it."

"I'm just standing in the river and taking things as they come in," said Linda.

ix

Savitri was very excited to hear about the encounter with the bookseller's daughter. She studied the various notes and concluded that they were all written by the holy man.

The cook had recovered from his bout of illness and had made vadas. These he brought to the balcony along with freshly brewed chai. The evening was balmy and conducive to conversation and the foursome took full advantage of it.

"I'm amazed at how everything in life circles back to its origin to make a new beginning. Consider these circularities: Gopal connects with a holy man who has moved into a burned-out house on Prayer Hill; Linda connects with Gopal; the holy man uses Gopal to connect Linda with Raman and Kumortuli; a train journey to Calcutta to visit Kumortuli connects Linda with my husband; and now, there is the connection to the bookseller's daughter. The center of all these circles, of course, is Mala Nagar. I think we'll soon find out what the new circles are."

Savitri paused in her analysis and took a deep breath before continuing. She pondered why the holy man didn't do things more directly,—why he took the long road to get things done.

"I don't think the holy man does anything in a calculated way, although I do believe he has knowledge of things and how they interface with each other," said Linda.

Raman disagreed in the gentlest way possible. He pointed to the two magazines that the holy man had passed on to Linda, which were responsible for their friendship and their trip to Kumortuli. "Those actions were very calculated," he said.

Rishi offered a more advanced theory by saying that holy men had forces surrounding them that influenced actions in the world. "Sometimes these forces operate independently of the holy men, but they are always connected," he said.

"Now I know why the holy man speaks only to Gopal," said Savitri. "He couldn't be a holy man if he had to listen to people spouting theories all day long."

"You were spouting theories yourself," complained her husband.

"I was making observations, dear," said Savitri, dismissively.

"Oh, have it your way."

The books that Linda had purchased were sitting on the table.

"How far is Midnapore from here?" she asked, picking up *Potters of Midnapore*.

"About 80 miles," said Savitri. "It's just north of Kharagpur, where my son goes to college."

"Look at this!" exclaimed Linda, holding up a business card. "I didn't see it here before."

The card read:

Pradip Roy's Bookshop
28 College Street
Calcutta 700009

New & used books
Trades welcome

They all took a look at the card, knowing they were touching something that had a special connection.

"Maybe we can stop there tomorrow morning before going to Kumortuli and the flower market," suggested Linda. Raman agreed to this plan.

It was not uncommon for a business card to be inside of a book, and it was agreed that Linda must have overlooked it when she was inspecting the books for precisely such an item.

The impact of these recent events and their reflection on matters involving the holy man were such that other topics waited in the wings for entry. Recognizing this, perhaps, Rishi steered the conversation toward the following day's agenda.

"You've come at a good time for going to Kumortuli," he said to Linda. "We are looking ahead to the puja months and a lot of images will be made from here on out. There was a time when all the clay used for making the images came by boat from the banks of the Hooghly, but today they come by lorry. Also, you could buy a ton of clay for 15 rupees,—today it'll cost you 300, maybe more."

"I'm looking forward to it," said Linda. "What fascinates me is the way the bamboo frame, straw, and clay come together to create these images. I saw some of that work in the town of Bijli, but it was on a much smaller scale. I can't wait for tomorrow!"

Linda paused for a moment, and then added, "It's sad that on immersion day, the clay is returned to the river,—all that hard work made tabula rasa."

"Look at it from the point of view of the artisans," said Savitri. "If there was no immersion, they would have no new orders for the following year."

"True," said Raman. "There's also a philosophical undercurrent to all of it—the idea of the transient nature of all things; ashes to ashes and dust to dust, as it says in the Bible. I read somewhere that in some cultures, people make elaborate patterns on the floor,—was it with flowers or powder?—and then cancel their effort by sweeping the work into a nondescript pile."

Savitri brought up kolam,—floor paintings made with rice flour, chalk, and colored pigments,—which decorate the front of homes and are made every morning.

"I was thinking of a ritual in the Buddhist tradition," said Raman.

"You're thinking about mandalas made with colored sand," added Rishi. He then quoted a few lines from *Elegy Written in a Country Churchyard* to drive home the point about the impermanence of all things.

"Oh, I love that poem,—one of my favorites," said Linda.

The conversation continued along these lines,—touching upon various aspects of culture, philosophy, and religion,—until it was time for dinner.

When everyone was seated at the table, Savitri tuned the radio to a station playing Rabindrasangeeth.

"This was our favorite song when we were much younger," said Savitri.

"It still is," corrected her husband, as *Ektuku Chhoan Lage* continued to play.

"We're not going to quarrel about that, are we?" asked Savitri, with a twinkle in her eyes.

x

What is it about books here that makes people go crazy, wondered Linda. In London's bookshops she had seen people engaged with books, but it was on a dignified, low-key level,—they stood in quiet corners perusing books. Here in College Street, though, people were going after books with a passion, as if they were gold or silver,—some precious commodity.

Linda and Raman made a beeline for Pradip Roy's Bookshop. They did not have the time to make any stops along the way, as they had a busy day planned at Kumortuli and the flower market.

The bookshop was a one-room affair, sandwiched between two other similar establishments. There was just enough room inside for a chair, a table, and two or three customers,—the rest of the space was covered by books. Linda noticed that two stacks of books were on the table as well. The College Street axiom was a simple one: space exists only to be filled by books.

The man sitting in the chair came out as soon as he saw Linda and Raman.

He said "namaste" and invited them inside to look at the books.

"We bought some books from your daughter yesterday," said Linda. "She took care of our needs quickly and efficiently."

"Yes, Priya, she's a jewel. She helps me a lot with my business. She has a sense about customers,—she can pick out people in a crowd who will buy books,—it's a gift."

Stepping inside the shop, Linda took a quick glance at the book titles. At eye level, in the middle of a stack, was a biography of Tagore, and right next to it, belonging to an adjacent stack, was a collection of stories by Pushkin. What caught her eye and held her interest was *The Sariwallah*. It was on top of a stack, sitting in an upright position, as though it was royalty.

"What's the price for this one?" asked Linda, holding up the book.

"Twenty-five rupees, madam, but you can get three books for 50 rupees. That's a better deal."

"Do you have any more books by this author?"

"Give me just two minutes," said the owner, and went running off to his right. He was back soon, with two books in his hand: *The Bus to Agra* and *A Touch of Miracle*.

"I think madam will enjoy these novels. He's an Indian writer, and all the stories take place in India."

"Thank you so much," said Linda. "And what is your daughter's name? Oh, never mind, you told us already,—Priya. Tell her that we came by. We'll try to visit one more time before we head back to Mala Nagar."

"Mala Nagar!" A look of incredulity swept over the owner's face. "My wife is from Mala Nagar, —in fact, she's in Mala Nagar right now, visiting her sister. This is quite a coincidence."

The owner took out a piece of paper from his pocket and scribbled down a name and an address and gave it to Linda. "Perhaps madam will say hello to my wife. She'll be surprised. Mala Nagar, of course, is no longer just an ordinary town. The holy man has changed all that,—I read about it in the papers."

"I'm making a documentary about the holy man," said Raman, "and Gopal,—I'm sure you read about him in the papers, as well,—is very close to us, and very close to the holy man."

They introduced themselves properly and talked for a while about the happenings in Mala Nagar. Linda brought up the Circularities Theory espoused by Savitri, and said to Pradip, "It seems like you're the next circle in the family of circles having their center at Mala Nagar." To add weight to this assertion, she produced from her purse the note that she had found inside the book.

"You see, don't you, that everything is connected. What looks like random meetings, random events, seem to have been well-oiled by the hand of destiny."

Pradip agreed and quoted some lines from Rumi. Then he added, "In the world of the mystic,—perhaps it's true of the holy man, as well,—distances exist without separation. What this means is that there are not many circles, but one. Once we recognize this truth, it is easy to see that the world is ablaze with God."

Linda clapped her hands. "You're something of a philosopher yourself," she said.

"When I was a young man, I had *The Essential Rumi* on my bookshelf," said Raman. "It was a birthday gift from my uncle. I wonder whatever happened to that book. I had it with me for years and years, and then it was gone."

He thought about the messages contained in the holy man's notes,—things spoken by the river, its conversations, its songs,—and continued, "Things stream into our lives and then stream out. While we are going about our daily business,—making a living, raising children, sending them to school, accumulating things, and climbing ladders,—a force unseen or unrecognized is subtracting time from our lives."

"Indeed," said Linda, "and if we don't make haste, we're going to find out that our Kumortuli trip has been subtracted from the day. We had better get going, Pradip. We promise to come back and have another nice long chat, and hopefully we'll get to see Priya again."

After saying goodbye, they had to walk a few blocks to get to the car. Ramnaresh was standing at the street corner and seemed to be having a spirited conversation with two men. Conversation is such an important aspect of the Calcutta way of life, thought Linda,—in fact, it was the signature aspect of the Indian way of life. Whether traveling by train or shopping at a store, one was bound to become entangled in a conversation,—and it could be about a Satyajit Ray movie, a cricket match, or potholes in the streets. The charm of the city was the voices of its people.

Ramnaresh dropped them off near the intersection of Rabindra Sarani and Durga Charan Banerjee St. No sooner had they gotten out of the car than a young man wearing a white Bengali-style dhoti and a beige kurta announced himself as their guide.

"Nearly 700 families live in the Kumortuli area," he said, with a casual confidence that promised more facts and figures to come. "I show madam everything."

"What about me?" asked Raman, a little tongue-in-cheek.

"Not to worry," came the assuring response. "Srikanth talks to everyone,—shows everyone everything there is to see." With that he surged ahead, and weaving his way through human traffic, bicycles, and carts,—and making several left turns and right turns,—brought them to a bylane which he proclaimed was the heart of Kumortuli. "Everything happens here," he said.

A cart carrying bamboo poles was parked against the wall, and two men were carrying a load on their shoulders to a shed nearby.

"That's where the frames are made,—" said Srikanth, "the best in Kumortuli. Come, I show you."

A man outside the shed was cutting the poles into smaller segments, while a man inside shaped them into proper length, width, and curvature to construct the frames. Finished frames occupied most of the floor space,—like the books in College Street, thought Linda,—leaving the man a small circular area in the middle for his work.

"This is where they make the smaller images,—of Ganesh, the demon, the buffalo, and the lion," explained Srikant. "A little down the lane is a much bigger shed where they're making larger images of the main gods and goddesses. We go there now."

A cart loaded with straw passed them by, followed by another cart loaded with clay. Some of the work of attaching the bamboo frames to wooden platforms was being performed outside. Linda was amazed at the narrowness of the lane and the tight spaces in which people were doing all the work. A young girl carrying a pail of water in each hand smiled at them.

"The binding of the straw to the frame is very important because you have to get the posture right," said Srikanth. "Then the straw structures are coated with clay."

They watched two men engaged in the work of straw-binding to create the framework for the demon and the lion. In an adjacent work area, a man was mixing chopped paddy stalk and clay by adding water, while another man stomped on the mixture to even it out. This mixture was then applied to the bound straw of the demon and the lion.

Srikanth proved to be an excellent guide. He took them to all the right places and showed them all aspects of the image-maker's trade, taking just the right amount of time at each stop to give their three-hour visit a comprehensive sweep. He answered all sorts of questions (why the four fingers of each hand were made using a mold, but the thumb had to be fashioned separately by hand); translated for them, as Raman did not speak Bengali; and established, with his community connections,—he seemed to know everyone,— lines of communication that otherwise might have proved difficult.

"How much do we owe you?" asked Raman, when the tour came to an end.

"Oh, I cannot accept any money," said Srikanth, drawing himself up to a full, self-righteous height. "I am the Community Manager for Kumortuli,—I'm an elected official."

"Why didn't you tell us before?" asked Linda, surprised by the revelation.

"It doesn't matter. I hope you enjoyed the tour," said Srikanth, in a very solemn tone.

"We sure did. Thank you so much."

On the taxi ride to the Mallick Ghat Flower Market, Linda thought about the artisans of Kumortuli working hard to eke out a living, while in her own country, artists were splashing paint on canvases to create modern art and making millions. "In most instances, there is no fairness in the scheme of things," she told herself. Then the image of the young girl carrying a pail of water in each hand flashed across her mind. In a crowded bylane of Kumortuli, where hope was fragile and tomorrow was uncertain, a young girl had given a smile to radiate happiness to others,—a gesture that, under the circumstances, was very generous. It was like the conversations in the river, thought Linda—simple, and full of grace.

She smiled to herself. At that very moment, Raman turned his face towards Linda to say something, and he caught that smile. That was enough,—its beauty, its weight, its reach, suddenly overwhelmed him, as a vista that appears in a scenic route to take the breath away. He knew then that he was in love with Linda.

xii

The revelation that he was in love with Linda having occurred rather suddenly, Raman now looked at her with new eyes and with a mind that was eager to decorate her with new attributes. He was engaged in these delectations of thought when the taxi came to a stop near the Howrah Bridge and the driver pointed towards the steps that would take them to the flower market.

The steps were slippery, and the path itself was muddy, having been trodden by thousands of feet since the market opened at four in the morning. The major transactions of the day had been completed already,—hoteliers, businessmen, temple representatives, and organizers of festivals, came early to get the freshest merchandise and the best prices,—and the crowd had thinned somewhat, but the place was still packed and full of noise and activity. The market was a parade of colors, stretching from the pristine, white austerity of lily, jasmine, and togor, to the dazzling flamboyancy of marigold and sunflower,—with an interlude of delicacy provided by rose and lotus blossom. Vendors sat behind baskets of flower arrangements and bouquets, while others walked about with long chains of jasmine and marigold hanging from their shoulders.

"I am a star fallen from the blue tent upon the green carpet…I am the memory of a moment of happiness," said Raman, quoting Khalil Gibran, as he bought a string of jasmine for Linda's hair. He actually bought a dozen strings,—dozen being the smallest unit of purchase at Mallick Ghat, —and carried them on his shoulder like the vendors did.

"You are so sweet," said Linda, beaming with joy. "I'll put it in my hair as soon as we get back to the house. I'll have Savitri help me."

Raman couldn't wait for the picture he had conjured up in his mind to come to fruition. He pictured Linda with her hair braided and pinned with an arrangement of jasmine. "She'll look as beautiful as some of the women in Pre-Raphaelite paintings," he told himself.

Linda encroached upon his reverie by saying that the metal structure of the Howrah Bridge in the background announced a different world, and the contrast it offered with the makeshift shelters next to the stalls where the vendors lived was sharp and striking.

"India is a land of contrasts at every turn, isn't it?" she remarked.

"Yes, yes," said Raman, his mind still distracted. He was thinking about how Linda stood in contrast herself,—an elegant, divine creature in the midst of so much disharmony and confusion. Even among the tightly packed crowd and in the middle of all the hustle and bustle, she walked in a light-footed way, as though she was skipping along through air; and when she turned her head and her tresses performed their dance, the melee in the marketplace was transferred to a theater's stage where an elegant, magical scene was being enacted.

"Yes, yes," repeated Raman, "India is full of contrasts…and contradictions."

They decided that they would come back to the market very early in the morning the next day, so Raman could conduct some interviews and get footage for his documentary.

"If you think this place is crowded now, wait till you see what it looks like tomorrow," he said.

Linda pictured Raman navigating his way through the crowd carrying his camera and tripod. "It's going to be a challenge for you with all the equipment," she said.

"We'll manage," he said, brushing off the concern, and Linda was pleased to be included as an integral part of the enterprise.

"I'll help you," she added.

Just then, a young man walked straight up to Linda and handed her a rose. "It's for luck; Madam is very beautiful," he said.

The gesture took a little bit of courage, she thought, especially as she was with a male companion, but before she could say a proper "thank you," the young man had melted back into the crowd.

"That was sweet."

"Cheeky, if you ask me," responded Raman.

"May we go back to Kumortuli tomorrow after the flower market?" asked Linda. "I think a second visit will firm up the impressions in my mind."

"Yes, let's do that, and I'll take some footage of the place as well, since I'll have my camera with me."

Recording, cataloging, making documentaries, writing books,—what do they accomplish in the end, wondered Linda. She thought about the holy man and how he had moved past all these trappings. This thought brought her mind back to Mala Nagar and she realized that she missed Gopal.

"A book, a photograph, or a clay image, is one thing, but a child is an entirely different proposition," she told herself. "Bring a child into the picture and the whole world changes."

"What are you thinking about?" asked Raman, noticing her pensive demeanor.

"Mala Nagar,—I was thinking about Gopal."

xiii

At the dinner table, Savitri felt sad that her newly acquired friends would be leaving the following day. Her sadness, however, was circumscribed because she knew that she would be catching a train to Mala Nagar as soon as she got word of the holy man's return to Prayer Hill.

"Since I'm a member of the family of circles, it's only fair that I should visit the center once and be part of all the happenings."

"Absolutely," said Linda, "and I hope you get to come very soon."

The conversation that ensued touched upon a broad range of topics. Rishi talked about his nephew who was leaving for America soon, and Savitri opined that there was no great advantage to an American education, positing that IIT Kharagpur was far superior to MIT any day. Linda pointed out that Indian academics was made sanguine by its no-nonsense approach, whereas colleges and universities in America and Europe frittered away too much time in sports and extracurricular activities.

"You can't get away from the fact that it was the Americans who put a man on the moon," said Rishi.

"And what good has it done for the people?" asked Savitri, trying to bait him into an argument.

"It's all about adventure and seeking new frontiers," countered Rishi. "I recall a famous line from a Tennyson poem,—To strive, to seek, to find, and not to yield."

"There you go again wandering off into a dubious area," said Savitri, with playful disdain. "Tell me, what has poetry accomplished? Absolutely nothing. It's as useless as a man on the moon."

Neither Linda nor Raman wanted to intercede during this exchange for fear that its theatricality would be lost or diminished.

"Poetry," said Rishi, assuming a grave tone, "brings us beauty and hope,—it produces transcendence."

"It accomplishes nothing," repeated Savitri, not budging from her position.

"Have it your way," conceded Rishi.

The conversational turf having been cleared of banter, Raman complimented the chana masala and the puri, and a consensus was reached about the cook being a treasure in the household.

Raman then talked about his parents' business and how it was being affected by the government's new monetary policy, and Rishi expounded on the "infernal" red tape that was a drag on his own foundation. "We must limit the reach and scope of government," he declared, with a fervor that could have belonged to a revolutionary.

Savitri chimed in right away with, "We need government, or we'll find ourselves ruled again by kings and tyrants."

Thus the badinage and regular conversation continued in cycles, much to the delight of Linda, who thought that Rishi and Savitri were a charming couple, despite their show of discord and contentiousness.

"You must write to me as soon as you've met the bookseller's wife," said Savitri. "I'm very curious to know how that story develops."

"I myself am looking forward to that meeting," said Linda. "These connections, these encounters, they're like a compass in my life,— showing me new things, taking me to new destinations."

xiv

The train was late and it was past ten o'clock,—so meeting Gopal had to wait till the next morning. Linda was disappointed, of course, but she was tired from all the journeying, and took kindly to the idea of going to bed and getting a good night's rest.

As she lay in bed, a melange of remembrances crowded her mind,—Kumortuli, the flower market, College Street, the Tollygunge mansion, and the playful banter between Rishi and Savitri,—but very quickly, sleep got the upper hand.

Raman came promptly at eight. He was dressed very formally—brown shoes, gray pants, long-sleeved blue shirt, tie, and brown jacket.

"I have to meet the producer of my documentaries this afternoon," he explained, sensing what was on Linda's mind.

"Let's go visit Gopal, and then shall we go to the tea stall for vada and chai?"

"Sounds good to me," said Raman.

Gopal must have been at the window and seen them coming up the road, for he rushed out of the house to greet them.

"It's been only four days, but it seems like such a long time!" said Linda, embracing Gopal. "What have you been up to, and how is school?"

Gopal understood the second part of the question and answered before Raman had to translate.

"Gopal good in school," he said, "make good work."

Once they were inside the house, he went directly to his school bag, which was sitting next to the table, pulled out a sheaf of papers, and handed them to Linda.

"I'm very proud of my boy," said his grandmother, placing a restraining hand on Gopal to curb his enthusiasm. "He can't wait to tell you all that has happened in the last few days, especially at school."

"See, master give A—top in class," said Gopal, proudly tapping his finger on the grade shown on the paper.

"Very good," said Linda. "I'm proud of your work. I'm also happy to see that your English has improved in just a few days."

Gopal brushed off his grandmother's hand from his shoulder and ran towards his school bag a second time. He took out two pieces of paper and brought them to Linda, his face streaked with excitement. The notes were in the holy man's hand, but they were written in Hindi.

"What does it say?" asked Linda, beside herself with anticipation. Had the holy man returned to the hill?

Raman translated. The first note was addressed to Gopal. It read:

Remember that even when your memsahib has to go away for a short time, she's still here with you,—just as I'm still on Prayer Hill when I'm not there.

Such is the power of love: it can be everywhere and all at once. Keep it with you always.

Do well in school.

Om

The second note was a drawing of seven concentric circles with the word "Om" written at their center.

Linda gasped. "How did he know about that?"

"Look!" exclaimed Raman. "There's a small arrow pointing away from the last circle, and at the end of it the word 'Om' is repeated."

Gopal thought the adults were making too much of a simple matter. The holy man liked drawing pictures,—that's all there was to it.

On the walk to the tea stall, Gopal skipped along beside Linda, playing host to all the distractions that came his way. He fed a goat from a remnant of food that was in his pocket; chased a few crows; and climbed a tree and leapt over some ditches in a daring exploit which involved chasing some dacoits in a forest to recover the king's jewels.

The tea-stall owner was happy to see them all. Whenever there was a lull in the business, he came over to their table and picked up tidbits about their trip. He found Savitri's Circularities Theory really interesting and had a lot to say about it.

"I know everything is connected, and I can be persuaded even to believe in destiny," he said, "but you're living through all of it, validating it,—that's what's amazing."

"There's more to it than that," interjected Raman. "The holy man is constantly reminding us that we are not defined by our physical presence alone. The mind is more powerful, and it can be made stronger through meditation and training. Who was it that said that at any given moment we use only two percent of our brain? That's where the holy man is different, I think. He uses a lot more of his brain and has discovered things we don't have a clue about."

Raman then turned to Gopal, who was busy putting away vada and jilebi, and explained that they were discussing the holy man's notes.

"He says a lot of fancy things, but I can draw better than him," said Gopal.

How much simpler is life when one is a child, thought Linda. A picture came to her mind of a child at a museum trailing after his mother,—purpose and purposelessness wedded together: the child content with the discovery of distractions, while the mother tries to push away distractions to get to the root of the matter, the meaning of the painting in front of her. The songs of childhood move with prism eyes, she concluded, and the leap of continents is achieved with little exertion.

xv

Linda was astounded to discover that she had met the bookseller's wife already, for she was none other than the woman who had approached her at Ashoka Restaurant on behalf of her ailing sister and wanted a necklace blessed by the holy man. It seemed that the Circularities Theory was announcing victory with trumpets and fireworks.

Sushmita Roy was equally surprised when everything was explained to her. She felt that all the connections were being established for a reason, except that she had no idea what it was.

"It's like a jigsaw puzzle for which we have only some of the pieces, so we have no idea what the final picture looks like."

"When I was living in London, I didn't even know these puzzle pieces existed," said Linda.

A faint voice came from the adjoining room.

"Let me see what Asha wants," said Sushmita. "Her asthma is acting up and that makes everything worse."

The vial of holy water that I gave didn't help her any, Linda thought to herself, but miracles can't happen at every turn in the road. Mother Mary appeared to St. Bernadette at the grotto in Lourdes, but only to her,—and miracles touched the lives of only a few people in that community.

Linda admired the set up of Indian homes,—its simplicity, its focus on comforts, and its utilitarian aspects. Just like in Italy,—a country she had visited many times,—where Mother Mary was ubiquitous and looked down on you from every building and every street corner, the living rooms of Indian homes showed that faith was central to daily life. A large framed picture of Shiva and Parvati was on the wall with a fresh garland of marigolds around it. Linda was also impressed by the reverence shown toward elders, especially parents. Two framed pictures of both parents also adorned the wall.

Sushmita returned to say that she may have to take Asha to the doctor if she got any worse.

"We don't want to be in your way," said Raman, solicitously, and then added, "but do let us know if we can be of any help."

"Thank you. She was doing fine just six months ago and then all this happened. Her husband Bala will be back from work around five o'clock. She does better when he's home with her."

"How long are you staying in Mala Nagar?" asked Linda.

"Maybe a week, maybe two weeks. I'm in no hurry to get back. My husband and Priya know how to manage the business and take care of the household. I do want to see the holy man before I leave."

"I have a sense he will be back soon,—it's just a feeling I have," said Linda, much to Sushmita's delight.

They talked for a little longer, and Sushmita promised to meet them again soon.

The second surprise of the day—no, better call it a shock—came when they were at the base of Praarthana Hill. A man had set up a table on the sidewalk and was handing out flyers while at the same time talking to people in a loud and booming voice.

"He's not a fan of the holy man,—" said Raman, and after listening to him a little longer, added, "as a matter of fact, he is denouncing the holy man as a fraud."

"You better be careful about what you're saying," shouted an elderly woman, shaking a stick at him, "or you may find yourself driven out of town on a donkey's back!"

"How dare you call the holy man a fraud. You're nothing but a scoundrel, a cheap scoundrel!" shouted a man, right in the troublemaker's face.

"I have a good mind to put you on a donkey and ride you out of town right now," said an energetic voice in the crowd.

The flyer was in Hindi and Raman did the translation for Linda. It announced a meeting near the Government House on Saturday at ten o'clock where a group of speakers was going to expound on the topic of fraud in religion. The organization issuing the flyer was The Philosophical Society for Universal Rationalistic Religion.

'You've been taken in by cheap tricks, all of you," said the agitator. "Give me a few hundred people on any given day and I'll show you something miraculous that happened to at least one of them. And don't talk to me about the rosebush,—someone switched out the dead one in the middle of the night."

The agitator surveyed the angry crowd and his eyes settled on Gopal.

"Oh, there's the boy that everyone is talking about,—the holy man's little puppet."

Gopal made a lunge at the man and started swinging his hands wildly. Linda rushed to his side and dragged him back. Gopal, however, was nimble and managed to break free, and reaching the agitator once more gave him a sharp kick in his leg. The crowd clapped and cheered. It took both Linda and Raman to drag Gopal back to a safe distance.

"I won't let him say bad things about the holy man!" protested Gopal, brimming with anger.

"You should control your child," scolded a middle-aged man, attired in western clothes, and Raman told him to mind his own business.

"You can't have your child running around like a little beast and kicking this man just because he wants to express an opinion," continued the critic.

"Maybe he'll kick *your leg* next," said a voice in the crowd.

Just then two policemen showed up on the scene and started to disperse the angry crowd. They recognized Gopal, and one of them said to Raman, "He's from Bijli. Some members of his group are also at the house. I wouldn't go there if I were you. There's going to be trouble."

"I'm not afraid of trouble," said Gopal, in a feisty tone. "Nobody is going to say bad things about my holy man. I'll show them what trouble is."

"Gopaaal," said Linda, and there was sufficient force in her voice and her look to calm the Little Warrior.

"Let's go see what's happening at the house," said Raman, and they started up the hill, with Linda holding Gopal's hand, and Gopal muttering vengeance upon all the enemies of the holy man.

xvi

On a patch of grass across from Government House, members of the PSURR had set up a long table for invited speakers and several folding chairs for people attending the event. When Linda and Raman got to the venue, about 30 people were milling about the area, some sipping chai from terracotta cups, while others were engaged in heated discussions. Two policemen kept their eyes on the proceedings. Anjali Dutt of the Daily Beacon was there, along with the paper's photographer Ramesh Pratap.

Linda spotted the man with whom they had had a confrontation standing behind the speaker.

"Look," she said, as Raman was steadying the tripod and making adjustments to his camera, "there's the man whom Gopal kicked in the leg. I'm glad we chose not to bring Gopal to this event."

The event was launched without any fanfare. The first speaker got up at the appointed hour and started addressing the crowd.

"I am Rohit Kapadia, president of the Philosophical Society for Universal Rationalistic Religion. I want to assure you that I am a religious man and so are all the people here with me."

"You're nothing but a university hack!" shouted a man, who was standing next to Raman. "Stick to teaching drama to your students,—we don't need any of your drama here."

Just then a group of men and women holding up signs in support of the holy man arrived on the scene.

"As I was saying," continued the speaker, recovering from the effect of the heckler's attack, "we are here in support of God and religion. What we don't want is the good name of Mala Nagar to become tarnished by a fraudster."

"Go back to Bijli," shouted a voice. "You're the big fraudster."

"Shaitan!" shouted a woman, standing next to him.

Undaunted, the speaker continued. "I want you to know that God is not in the business of doing conjuring tricks. You don't need miracles to point the way to God,—all you need to do is look at a sunrise, look at a lotus blossom."

The speakers at the table and supporters in the crowd clapped their hands.

"A wicked and adulterous generation seeketh after a sign, and there shall no sign be given unto it. That's from the Bible. You see, all the religions of the world uniformly oppose holy men who perform cheap tricks."

"Are you calling us wicked?" demanded an angry voice. Someone launched a tomato in the direction of the table. It whizzed past the speakers and struck a tree behind them.

"And whom are you calling adulterous?"

The policemen switched their stance from casual to aggressive by displaying their lathis more prominently.

"Should we leave? I think a fight is going to break out," whispered Linda to Raman.

"We're OK for now. You stand behind me. We'll retreat quickly if things start to get out of hand."

"Your holy man is no holy man," continued the speaker. "Why, I've seen better tricks at a cheap magic show."

"He has put Mala Nagar on the map. He's good for business. He has cured people's diseases. What have you done for us?" The voice belonged to a woman.

What the speaker said next could not be heard because a new group of supporters of the holy man, chanting and beating on drums, drowned out the speech.

The man sitting to the speaker's right had had enough. He got up from his chair violently, walked to the end of the table, picked up a pail of water that was sitting there, and threw it on the saboteurs.

This sudden act froze the scene momentarily. Raman picked up his tripod, took Linda's hand, and walked away to the other side of the road. The policemen swung into action, but two of them were not enough for the melee that followed.

The crowd charged the table and toppled it. A few of the speakers found themselves on the ground, the president of the PSURR being one of them.

Assuming the vertical, and swinging a walking stick in gratuitous defense, he blamed the holy man for the crisis.

"He'll pay for this," he threatened. "He's going to need a miracle to escape the wrath of Rohit Kapadia!"

"What an adventure," said Linda, from their safe distance. "I never thought I'd see anything like it. I'm glad you've got most of it on film. It'll be fun to watch it later and pick up all the little bits we might have missed in real time."

The meeting that started somewhat contentiously devolved into a free-for-all, reported the Daily Beacon. *The speakers' corner threw a pail of water on the protestors, and the latter retaliated by overturning the table and upending the speakers. The scene was reminiscent of a brawl in a Laurel and Hardy movie. We wonder if the holy man—wherever he is—has any idea of the amount of mischief he has caused in absentia, in a once-sleepy town.*

"We can't have all this action taking place and the holy man not be here," said Linda. "It's funny how just a week ago there was not even a whisper of opposition to him, and suddenly, out of the blue, we have a war waging between two parties."

"Funny, indeed," said Raman. "I wonder what else is going to come unannounced, without a whisper, and take us by surprise."

xvii

Gopal returned from school, had a quick bite to eat, washed the food down with some buttermilk, and went out to play. When it was eight o'clock and there was no sign of him, his grandmother started to get worried. Now that Gopal was in school, he had curtailed his late-night, outdoor activities with his friends. Also, there was the matter of homework, and he had shown himself to be very responsible in meeting his academic obligations. So what was keeping him? By nine o'clock, his grandmother was in a fitful state, and decided to seek help. Her first instinct was to contact the police, but on her way to the station, she decided to stop first at Linda's apartment.

Linda was surprised to hear a knock on her door at this late hour,—and more surprised to find Gopal's grandmother standing there, looking very troubled and agitated, and speaking in a tone that pointed to a crisis. Gopal's name was mentioned a few times, and Linda surmised that something was the matter with her grandson.

Main Street in Mala Nagar was busy even late at night, and Linda knew that she would find someone to do the translating for her. The very first person she encountered—a man who appeared to be in his mid-twenties—was more than willing to help.

"We must go to the police," said Linda, as soon as she was apprised of the facts. "We must go right away,—there's no time to lose." Then turning to the man, she asked, "Will you find a rickshaw for us?"

The man took off running, and Linda went up to her apartment to fetch her purse. It wasn't long before the man returned riding in a cycle rickshaw.

"Police station jhaana hai. Jhaldi chalo!" said Linda, helping the grandmother onto the vehicle.

All kinds of crazy thoughts passed through her mind and she tried to push them away. "He couldn't have been in an accident," she told herself, "otherwise someone would have reported it. Could it be that he went to the hill? But why would he do that,—the holy man was not there. Maybe the holy man has come back. The police will find out, they'll tell us."

The rickshaw ride seemed to have calmed down the grandmother a little, but she still kept talking to herself and to Linda. Knowing the circumstances, the rickshaw driver pedaled furiously and got them to the police station in record time.

The clerk inside was enjoying his peace and quiet, and reading a magazine, when Linda and the grandmother burst into the room. They both spoke at the same time, and there was so much animation and urgency in their voices that the sergeant stepped out of his office to find out what the commotion was about.

"What's gong on?" he demanded, and then recognizing Linda, added, "Ah! Gopal's guardian. What brings you here at this late hour?"

The grandmother found the inspector's congeniality quite offensive, considering the seriousness of the occasion. She ran to him, grabbed his shirt sleeve, and said quite vehemently, "You've got to find Gopal. I'm sure he's in some kind of trouble. You've got to find him right away!"

"I've got to have facts," said the sergeant, unable to shake off the grandmother's firm grip. "Please come into my office, sit down, and tell me everything you know."

After all the facts were laid out on the table, the sergeant said that he would drive around town in his jeep and see what he could find out. Linda asked if she could go with him, but he dismissed that suggestion as "not a sound idea."

" I think Gopal has been kidnapped," said the grandmother.

"Now what makes you say that?" returned the sergeant.

"He's got enemies," said the grandmother. "I heard about the man who tried to fight him,—people who don't like the holy man, people who don't like my grandson."

"I am aware of that situation. I'll interview all those people tomorrow morning and see what they have to say."

"You should go talk to them right now," said the grandmother. "If they have kidnapped my grandson, there's no telling what will happen to him before morning!"

"We don't have any real evidence for me to do that," remonstrated the sergeant. "We will get to the bottom of it, one way or another. If it is any comfort to you, I honestly don't think Gopal has been kidnapped."

"I do think it is something serious, though," fretted Linda.

"Yes, perhaps, but we hope not."

The sergeant dropped off his two visitors at the grandmother's house, where Linda had agreed to spend the night. He promised that he would inform them right away if he came into possession of any news.

"Gopal is the holy man's friend. He's sure to protect him," said the sergeant.

Linda thanked him profusely for that sentiment, for it gave her great comfort.

"Yes," she said to herself. "I hope he is able to protect him."

xviii

"We have intensified our search efforts," said Sergeant Praveen Bedi. "The police in Bijli and Jilpur are also cooperating with our efforts. But there's no sign of Gopal so far; no one appears to have seen him after 6 P.M. That's a little strange considering how Gopal is known for being out and about in the streets in the late evenings. I talked to his best friend—his gilli danda partner—and he said that he didn't see him last evening at all."

"You don't think he's gotten kidnapped, do you?" asked Linda, looking very worried. She had had only two hours of sleep, and the fatigue she felt made the situation seem bleaker than before.

"We cannot rule out that possibility," said the sergeant, changing his earlier stance in the matter.

"There was a fair amount of animosity shown toward him by one member of the PSURR. He called him the holy man's puppet. I bet he had something to do with it," said Raman.

"It's a little hard for me to imagine that a young boy has adult enemies," posited Linda, "but anything is possible, I suppose."

Slowly, a small group of people formed near the table to eavesdrop on the conversation. A woman carrying a shopping bag in each hand stopped to inquire after Gopal, and said that she would say a prayer for him when she visited the temple later in the afternoon.

"Let's look at the situation logically," chimed in the tea-stall owner, bringing Linda and Raman a cup of chai. "Gopal wouldn't disappear for a lark, and he wouldn't stay out late because he takes school seriously. No one saw him after 6 P.M., and the holy man is not in the picture right now. So, someone is holding him against his will,—and that amounts to kidnapping. But who's behind this outrage? Let's assume that the PSURR has a role in it. What's the motive? Maybe they want to show that the miracle-making power of the holy man is not enough to rescue the young boy. The story of Gopal's disappearance will be in all the newspapers tomorrow and everyone will know about it, including the holy man. Surely, a man who can make a dead rosebush bloom and shake a girl out of her coma should be able to locate a kidnapped boy and save him from captivity. I think that's the game,—they want to expose him as a fraud. Granted it's a crazy scheme, but there you have it."

Sergeant Bedi's mind was looking at various possible scenarios. He was trying to connect whatever dots were available to him.

"If he was kidnapped, he was either taken by force or lured into captivity. I'm going to rule out the former, because that's a risky undertaking. On the other hand, I can easily see someone like Gopal being taken in by a clever bait. I have policemen scouring the outskirts; they're looking at farm houses, abandoned buildings, isolated structures, and all the rest. And now, I must be off. I promised his grandmother that I'd stop by this morning and give her an update. After that, my next stop is Bijli, to see if the police chief there has any leads."

Not long after the sergeant left, Anjali Dutt joined them at their table.

"We have our reporters in Bijli and Jilpur on high alert," she said. "They're following every story that has a Gopal connection."

"What do you make of the whole situation?" asked Linda.

"Well, to be honest with you" said the stalwart reporter, "I don't think the situation has anything to do with the holy man or the group that opposes him. It's foolish to think a few adults—some of them affiliated with the university—would kidnap a child to make an academic, religious point. Here's what I told myself: everyone's attention is on Gopal, and this gives someone or some entity the cover to conduct some nefarious activity."

"That's a smart observation," said the tea-stall owner. "Did you mention that to the sergeant?"

"I did, but he didn't react to it in any particular way. He said simply that the police were considering all possibilities."

"What kind of nefarious activity could be going on here?" asked Raman. "It's not like this is a crime capital."

"Lot of things go on in quiet places," chimed in the tea-stall owner. After a slight pause, he continued, "Gopal is a resourceful chap, though, and he's also street-smart. He's not likely to take things lying down."

"And they better give him his daily ration of sweets," added Raman, "or he is likely to start a revolution singlehandedly."

He was trying to relieve the tension in a stressful situation, but he wanted to make sure that Linda understood his motive,—so he took her hand under the table ever so gently.

Linda felt the gentle touch of his hand, and her mind went back immediately to the previous afternoon when he had taken her hand near the Government House to move her to safety on the other side of the street. She also remembered how when they were at the flower market, he had taken her hand going down some wet, slippery steps.

She looked at him and smiled, letting him know that the joke was fine.

Poor Gopal, thought Linda. I wonder where he is, and who's feeding him and taking care of him. I better go and see how his grandmother is getting on. I said I would check back with her soon.

"Courage," she told herself. "Be strong. Things will work out in the end."

xix

It was almost five-thirty and Gopal was headed back home. He was thirsty, he had more homework than on the previous day, and the warning of his English master that all good boys should be at their studies by six still rang in his ears. It was just then that an auto-rickshaw coming at a high speed pulled up from behind him. Gopal was surprised by the sudden manifestation of the vehicle, and even more so by the voice of the driver exploding with urgency.

"The holy man has returned and your memsahib is on the hill with her friend. She asked me to come and fetch you. It's something very important!"

"Let me go tell my grandmother," said Gopal.

"There's no time to waste. Memsahib ordered me to bring you to the hill right away. We must go now!"

Gopal hopped onto the auto-rickshaw and the driver took off. After traveling on Main Street for about a mile, he took a sudden left onto a narrow, deserted lane.

"Why are we turning here?" asked Gopal.

"The hill is packed with people. Something very important is going on. I'll take the back roads to avoid all the traffic."

They had gone but a few hundred yards when the rickshaw came to a stop because a truck was blocking their way. It had its engine running.

"What are they doing parking a truck in this lane?" muttered the driver. He got out and started walking towards the truck.

He returned right away with two men at his side.

Something is wrong with this picture, thought Gopal, but he had no time to react. All three men grabbed him and carried him to the truck. Gopal couldn't scream because one man had his hand clamped firmly over his mouth.

The back of the truck was fitted with a metal frame that was covered with tarpaulin. One man flung the flap of tarpaulin onto the roof, got into the back of the truck, while the driver of the auto-rickshaw and the other man handed Gopal to him.

"Bachao! Bachao!" shouted Gopal, as the man's rough hand temporarily came off of his mouth.

The lane was dark and deserted. Gopal only hoped that someone had heard his cry. The driver of the auto-rickshaw returned to his vehicle and the truck took off.

It was him against two burly men in the back of the truck and the odds were not in his favor at all. He would have to be on the lookout for an opportune moment to do something,—maybe attempt an escape. Gopal was a veteran of many battles,—he had fought against mighty kings and cruel dacoits, and he had always emerged victorious. He started thinking like a general.

He started paying attention to the sounds the tires made against the ground. He smelled the air that made its way into the tarpaulin-covered enclosure. He also tried to keep a running estimate of the time of travel.

They must be on the road to Bijli or Jilpur, thought Gopal, because the truck was moving at a good pace. There was a railroad crossing on the way to Bijli, so he had to be alert for the sound the tires would make as they went over the tracks.

Gopal speculated that he must be more important than he thought he was, for otherwise why would these men be interested in him. Maybe they found out that he was going to build a palace one day on Praarthana Hill; or, maybe they wanted to lay claim to the trophy he was sure to win as the gilli danda champion of the world—a trophy made of gold and speckled with precious stones.

What advice would memsahib give him? He remembered that she never got ruffled. "That's the way I've got to be,—" he told himself, "calm and collected."

The truck was still going at a good speed and the tarpaulin was flapping against the rails of the frame. He took out the catapult that he always carried in his pocket and very casually let it fall out of the truck. He was fond of the catapult,—it had been instrumental in securing him victory in many battles,—and he was loathe to let it go. The two men were busy talking to each other in hushed voices. Gopal took off one of his shoes and dropped it out of the truck as well. He waited a little longer and did the same with the other shoe.

Just then, the truck went over the rail tracks. So they were on the road to Bijli. He knew exactly where they were. In a mile or so, they would be reaching a group of shops on the right. What should he do? Was there an opportunity here…should he call out for help?

The man sitting closer to him seemed to have read his mind. "You'll keep your mouth shut if you know what's good for you," he warned.

"I'm not afraid of you," said Gopal.

The man did not like this cheeky response and used his hand as a muzzle for a second time. When the truck had gone past the shops, the hand was removed and the men returned to their whispered conversation. Gopal caught a few words here and there but they didn't make any sense to him.

Gopal restarted his mental clock.

They must have gone another five miles or so when the truck made a left turn onto what sounded like a dirt road. Gopal realized his tactical blunder: this is where he should have tossed his second shoe. He let that thought go,—there was no point agonizing over that decision.

What would Gopal, the mighty emperor, do in these circumstances? "In strength I'm beaten, but not in mind," he told himself.

After a few minutes, the truck came to a stop. "Don't try anything foolish," warned the man, who had used his hand to silence him. "No one can hear you."

The men blindfolded him and took him out of the truck. It was definitely a dirt road. Then Gopal heard a door creak open. It must be an outside door, he thought, since it was so close to the road. They walked a short distance, and then the two men guided him up some steps. Another door creaked open. This must be the main door to the building, shed, or whatever it was. A dog barked in the distance. Is it possible he was on a farm?

Once inside, the blindfold was removed.

It *was* a shed, and it did belong to a farm, for there was some farm equipment leaning against the wall. A single light bulb hung from the ceiling and cast a pale yellow glow all around. In the light, Gopal saw that one of the men had a scar on his cheek, which made his face look very sinister.

"You keep first watch," said the scar-faced man, "and I'll go get us some food." Then turning to Gopal, he said with a scowl, "Don't try any of your fancy tricks. There are two watch dogs outside, and my man here has got a pistol,—he gets itchy with it sometimes."

"I'm not afraid of a pistol,—my army has got cannons," Gopal said to himself. He was about to say something cheeky but then he stopped, for on the wall opposite—the men were facing away from it—appeared the letter "Om", alongside a rose. The image flashed on the wall like a neon sign, and then disappeared.

The odds just got changed: it was no longer two against one. In the dimly-lit shed, Gopal drew himself up to his full height, put on his crown, marshaled his troops, and got ready to do battle.

Gopal was getting tired of his captivity.

"Where's my sweet?" he demanded, when the scar-faced man brought him his breakfast, which consisted of one oothappam, one vada, and a glass of milk.

"What you'll be getting, if you don't watch it, is a slap across your face," said the scar-faced man.

"I have a sweet with all my meals," persisted Gopal. "You'll be charged with kidnapping, but also starving a child."

The other captor came into the shed whistling a tune and shut the door quickly.

"Did you sleep well?" he asked, in a mocking tone.

"Like a king," replied Gopal, showing no sign of the discomfort he had suffered while sleeping upon a sheet on a hard, uneven floor. He then added, "You won't be whistling when they catch you and throw you in prison."

If I didn't have my instructions, I would knock some sense into that brat's head, thought his captor.

Gopal thought about the sign that had appeared on the wall. What did that mean? The holy man had said to him on numerous occasions that he could be in different places at the same time,— like a magician. So, why hadn't he showed up? What was he waiting on? He too thinks like a general, concluded Gopal,—that has to be it. He is waiting for the right, dramatic moment.

A dog barked outside. Soon, a second dog joined the act.

"Go see what it is," said the scar-faced man.

The door opened, closed, then opened again. The kidnappers were being very careful not to let Gopal get a look outside.

"It's a man on a bicycle."

"Well, go see what he wants. If he asks any questions, tell him we're here fixing the shed."

The man waiting outside the gate was tall and lean. His hair was disheveled, he had a scraggy beard, and he was dressed in dirty clothes. His complexion was sallow and it looked like he could use a meal.

"What do you want?" asked the kidnapper.

"I was just riding through, enjoying the day. Do you live here?"

"No, I'm working on the shed."

"It needs a coat of paint," said the bicyclist, "and maybe some repair to the roof. I want you to do something for me. I ran into a little swirl of dust as I rode up this path, and I think something got into my eyes. Take a look at them, will you?"

It was an odd request and the man obeyed without giving it any thought. As he peered into the bicyclist's eyes, a sudden feeling of dizziness came over him, and a weakness traveled down to his legs. He felt a desperate need to look away, to break contact with the bicyclist, but he was not able. Finally, his legs gave way, and he slumped to the ground.

The bicyclist walked to the shed and tried the door handle, but it was locked. He knocked on the door.

"Who is it?" shouted the scar-faced man.

"Your friend asked me to come and get you. He's trying to fix my bicycle and he needs your help."

The scar-faced man opened the door, looking displeased, and muttering something under his breath.

As soon as the door opened, the bicyclist pushed his way inside, and shouted "police!" The scar-faced man dropped the cup he was holding in his hand, and made a dash for the back door.

"It's you!" exclaimed Gopal, recognizing the homeless man from the riverbank. "How did you manage to find me here?"

"All in good time," said the homeless man. "Right now we need to get out of here quickly. We're going to take my bicycle all the way to your house."

"You're not a policeman, are you?" asked Gopal, his face glowing with excitement.

"Of course not, but they don't know that."

"I was expecting to get rescued, but not by you," said Gopal, as they walked briskly towards the gate.

The homeless man may have looked frail but he made the bicycle sing with his furious pedaling.

"I don't want to waste any of your time. You have a lot of people worried about you,— so you better go and talk to all of them," he said, dropping Gopal off in front of his house. "Come and see me at the riverbank, and we'll have a nice, long chat. And don't forget to bring me some food,—I'm always hungry."

Gopal blinked his eyes and pinched himself, as he watched the homeless man ride away on his bicycle. Was all of this really happening? Yes, it was. "The king has returned to his castle," he told himself.

xxi

Ganesh Tea Stall was definitely in the limelight that evening. Everyone connected with Gopal and his adventures was there, including the media. Anjali Dutt of the Daily Beacon was talking to Gopal and trying to capture all the details of his abduction and his subsequent dramatic rescue. A reporter from Hamara Desh Television Network—an affiliate of the newspaper chain— was recording the interview as well.

"So what happened after the door opened?" asked Anjali.

"The undercover detective stormed in, and I flung myself at the kidnapper. He knew the game was up, and ran out the door." Gopal spoke with bravado, and there was a sparkle in his eyes that lent itself to a suspicion that the story was being embellished and exaggerated.

Recognizing this, Anjali said, "I spoke with Sergeant Bedi, and he told me that none of his men took part in the rescue operation."

"Of course,—" said Gopal, "the man who saved me is not part of the police force. He's an undercover detective. He goes around in disguise as a homeless man."

"Where can we find him?"

"By the river bank," answered Gopal.

A reporter was interviewing Gopal's grandmother. This was the first time she had been interviewed by anyone, and the fact that reporters were waiting in line to ask her questions seemed to have unnerved her somewhat.

"Gopal is a very smart boy," she told them all. "He's also very brave. I'm very proud of him."

"What can you tell us about the sign that he saw in the shed?"

"Has he seen any other signs?" asked another reporter. "Has it anything to do with the holy man?"

"Why the rose? What do you think it means?"

"Gopal and the holy man connect in a special way. You will recall that my grandson played a part in the miracles. I think the rose is like his signature. He also put it on the notes that he sent to Shrimati Linda."

A large group of people had formed a semicircle around the reporters, and many of them were watching the proceedings with a keen interest, hoping that the television camera would catch them in its frame.

Linda and Raman sat at a table sipping chai and exchanging words with the owner.

"It was very clever of Gopal to throw his catapult and shoes out of the truck,—very strategic of him," said Raman.

"He'll be a military man before he becomes an architect," opined the owner.

"He said he missed his sweets, so I bought him a box of assorted sweets,—laddu, jilebi, barfi, and all the rest," said Linda. "He was in heaven. He gave me a big hug."

Just then Sergeant Bedi showed up in his jeep. No sooner had he gotten out of the vehicle than he was surrounded by a swarm of reporters hurling questions at him.

"Before I answer any of your questions," said the sergeant, "I want to put some rumors to rest. No, we did not have anything to do with the rescue operation; and no, the man who rescued Gopal is not part of law enforcement. The man who got Gopal out of the jam is a homeless man you've seen around these parts, often near the bank of the Poornima River. How he managed to find Gopal, I don't know; so don't ask me any questions about it."

"Have your spoken to the homeless man?" asked a reporter. "How come he's not around? How come we can't find him?"

"Do you know who the kidnappers are?" asked Anjali. "Why did they want to kidnap Gopal? Are they still on the loose?"

"I can't answer many of your questions because the investigation is ongoing. Also, more than the two kidnappers, we are interested in the person or persons who were orchestrating the event. Trust me, we'll get to the bottom of all this very soon."

"Gopal told us that he saw a sign in the shed just before his rescue. Do you think there was divine intervention? Do you think the holy man played a part in it?"

"I deal in facts," responded Sergeant Bedi.

"Well, it's a fact that Gopal saw the sign," persisted the reporter.

"How can you call it a fact? There's no corroboration. For the sake of argument, let's say he saw a sign. What of it? How does that help us with the investigation? I can tell you that—just to be on the safe side—I'm assigning a security detail to Gopal for the next few days. We hope to have this case wrapped up in the very near future."

Sergeant Bedi then approached Gopal's grandmother. "With your permission, I would like to take Gopal with me to our headquarters. He can help us in our work. He'll be back within the hour."

"So you have the two men in custody," said Linda. "You need him to identify them, is that it?"

"You're a very smart woman," said the sergeant, but he did not elaborate.

After Gopal and the sergeant had left, Anjali turned her attention to the owner of the tea stall.

"You hear all the stories and all the gossip surrounding Mala Nagar. What's your take on Gopal's rescue? Do you think the holy man had a hand in it?"

The owner was having a busy and profitable day. People were wanting biscuits, vadas, samosas, —and chai, of course. Several other items had sold out. He answered from behind the counter, "I used to be a skeptic about the holy man, but so many extraordinary things have happened. I think the holy man's hand is all over this incident."

xxii

The photo of Gopal standing next to Sergeant Bedi at the police headquarters made the front page of all the regional newspapers. Gopal presented a pleased, self-congratulatory demeanor and looked for all the world like a youthful hero. Linda purchased a copy of all the different newspapers for her collection.

"One day we will look back on this day and it will be fun to read all these stories," she told Raman, as they walked Gopal to school.

Their conversation was frequently interrupted as people walked up to Gopal to congratulate him, shake his hand, and pat him on the head. It was evident that he enjoyed all the adulation because he held his head high and walked with a swagger.

The principal was waiting near the school gate and posed with Gopal for pictures. He enjoyed the spotlight himself, and said to the reporters, "His first day back in school—that should make the front page as well."

Seeing Linda standing there with all the newspapers in her hand, a man said to her, "Funny they can't find the homeless man. His picture belongs on the front page as well. The reporters will have a field day with him if he should show up."

"It's very mysterious indeed," agreed Raman.

"My wife thinks the homeless man and the holy man are one and the same," said their interlocutor. "Stands to reason, considering that the sign appeared to Gopal in the shed right before his rescue. We can rule out this possibility if the two men were ever seen in the same place together, but that has never happened. What do you think?"

"Gopal has expressed to us that very same idea," said Linda. "I think it is farfetched myself, based on their different ages and looks. Gopal contends that the homeless man is the holy man in disguise. A clever disguise, if that is true."

"I wonder if we will ever find out," said the man. "I still think it is strange that the homeless man seems to have disappeared after such a dramatic rescue."

"That is strange," agreed Linda.

"By the way, my name is Bose—Dilip Bose. I'm a farmer from Jilpur."

"What kind of farmer?" asked Raman, after introducing himself and Linda.

"Oh, I grow all kinds of things—mostly jackfruit, tamarind, mango, and coconut. I'm trying to expand my business to Mala Nagar,—that's why I'm here. Of course, this town has a new identity. It has become synonymous with miracles."

"Yes," said Raman. "People are calling this place Miracle of the Rose."

"What do you think about the group that is opposing the holy man? I heard that its members are going to hold another meeting, this time in front of the library."

"I think they're just a bunch of attention seekers," said Linda. "I think people should just ignore them, and then they'll go away."

The second bell sounded to announce that classes were now in session. The policeman who had walked behind them on their way to the school, approached them, and said, "I'll keep an eye on the boy,—so you don't have anything to worry about."

"I'm going to the hill," said Dilip. "Would you care to join me?"

The day was laid out nicely, and they accepted the invitation.

On the way, a hand-drawn open cart passed by them carrying mounds of used flowers. Linda knew it was headed for the Poornima River, for it was believed that flowers used in worship were sacred and should be made one with the river, and not thrown into trash bins. In the end, everything returns to the river, to Ganga Ma, Linda thought. Even Gandhi Ji's body was given back to the Ganges,—that's why the holy man said that the river carries all our conversations.

"How I've changed," she said to herself. "I'm starting to think like an Indian."

Amazingly, there was still a line starting at the base of the hill, and two policemen were on duty to regulate traffic and maintain order. People were always willing to treat Linda and Raman in a special way,—being Gopal's guardians,—but they decided to stand in line with the rest of the people.

"Can you imagine what this place will be like when the holy man returns?" asked Dilip. "It'll be a madhouse. They'll need ten times the number of police to keep things calm and orderly."

Since the holy man was not there, people just wanted to walk by the house, and the line moved quickly.

When they got in front of the house, Linda asked the policeman standing guard if he had seen the holy man at all.

'There's no sign of him. We did find this note on the floor this morning. It is addressed to Gopal, but it is blank."

Linda took the note from him and studied it. It was a piece of paper folded in half and carried no message. She put it away in her purse and was looking over the policeman's shoulder when she saw the sign. There was no mistaking it,— the letter "Om" flashed on the door, just once, and then it was gone.

"Did you see it?" asked Linda, hardly able to contain her excitement.

"See what?"

"I just saw the holy man's sign on the door! It flashed just as Gopal had described it."

Both Raman and Dilip were dumbfounded, but they had not been looking in that direction at that time and could not offer any corroboration.

"What do you think it means?" asked Raman.

"I have no idea. And the blank note,—that's a mystery too."

It was later in the morning, when they were enjoying a cup of chai at Ganesh Tea Stall, that Linda discovered that the note she had put into her purse was folded not in half but in thirds.

"I don't believe it!" cried Linda. "Look at it! This note is folded in thirds. When we looked at it, it was folded in half."

"How could both of you have missed an extra fold?" asked the owner.

"Dilip looked at it too," said Raman. "There was nothing in the note,—only Gopal's name on the front."

Linda read out loud what was written on the extra fold.

Come and see me Saturday morning.
Om

"He's back!" she shouted. "He's back!"

xxiii

After leaving the tea stall, Linda and Raman decided to look in on Sushmita. The bookseller's wife greeted them warmly, and told them that Asha's health had taken a turn for the worse.

"I was meaning to come and see you, but things have been difficult here. I wish the holy man would come back. I think my sister needs his blessing very badly."

"He *is* coming back!—" said Linda, "this Saturday, as a matter of fact."

The drawn and troubled look on Sushmita's face disappeared and was replaced by a chipper expression.

"Oh, bless you for bringing me this good news," she said, deeply moved. "What a lovely surprise! Now I have to figure out a way to get Asha to the house on the hill."

"We'll give you a hand," said Raman. "Maybe we can get a wheelchair. The path up the hill is rough in places, especially near the top, but I think we'll be able to manage it."

"Oh, you're both angels, How did you find out he was coming back?"

"There was a note left for Gopal asking him to come and visit him." Linda then explained the peculiarities of the note and how she had seen the holy man's sign on the door.

"I'll make a flower garland for the holy man and hang it on his door," said Sushmita, quite excited about the prospect of a visit to the abandoned house.

"Bring me flowers with a loving heart and I will accept it, says Lord Krishna in the Bhagavad Gita. It can be fruits, or even water,—the key is that the giver's heart be pure," said Raman.

"The holy man mentioned that in one of his notes, didn't he?" said Linda.

"He did, indeed."

Saturday morning came on the back of great anticipation. Gopal was jumping around with excitement and couldn't wait to see the holy man after such a long absence. Linda had put together a basket of fruit to take to the house.

Raman had procured a wheelchair and Bala was pushing his wife,—she looked rather weak and sat slumped in the chair.

When they got to the base of the hill, they noticed that the line was a little longer than usual. Is it because it is a Saturday, or have the locals got wind of the holy man's return, wondered Linda.

"I come here every day hoping to see the holy man," said an elderly woman, who was standing in front of them in the queue.

"Maybe today will be the lucky day," said Raman, his voice full of knowing optimism.

As expected, the path was difficult to navigate in places, and Raman and Bala had to lift the wheelchair over some rough patches.

Gopal had moved ahead of the line. His presence on the hill was met with approval and positivism, and some people cheered him as he passed by.

"Make the holy man come back," uttered an old man, who was moving forward supported by crutches.

Gopal was a boy who liked theater and any opportunity that came his way to act with bravado. He seized upon the present moment, whose outcome was predetermined to be positive.

"Don't you worry," he said, with an expansive sweep of his hand, "I'll make the holy man come back."

The old man was not expecting such a robust response. "Will you?" he asked.

"You wait and see,—I'll make the holy man come back!"

"That boy knows something," said a woman, who was standing next to the man with crutches. "He and the holy man are very close. He was very positive about the holy man coming back. I believe him." With that she started singing, and a few neighboring people in line picked up the chant.

"Let everyone know the holy man is coming back," said someone in the crowd, and the news traveled quickly up and down the line.

When the word reached Linda, she turned to Raman, and said, "I told him not to say anything to people about the holy man coming back. I don't think he'd break his promise, do you?" It was a rhetorical question, for she continued by saying, "It wouldn't make any difference, anyway."

Singing picked up in other parts of the line. People who had brought drums started beating them, and those who had brought bells started ringing them.

News traveled faster than Gopal's two legs, and so the people who received the happy tidings ahead of his advance saw something prophetic when he came into their view.

"Look, Gopal is here!" shouted a woman. "Gopal is here!"

A man equated the boy's breakneck pace with a meeting in the offing, and cursed the line for moving so slowly.

When Gopal got to the front of the house, Anjali Dutt of the Daily Beacon was waiting for him. The television crew of Hamara Desh was also there.

"Come here, Gopal. Before you go in, I have a few questions to ask you."

Gopal loved reporters, and he took very kindly to the idea of being interviewed in front of a television camera. He assumed the air of a celebrity and approached Anjali.

"Is it true the holy man is returning to the house today? What can you tell us about it?" she asked.

He wanted very badly to be the purveyor of breaking news, but he remembered his promise to Linda. He had promised the man with the crutches that he would make the holy man come back, but that was not the same as revealing the contents of the note that he had received.

"I come here everyday," he said, taking a defensive tack. "The holy man is always here. He never left. That's why all these people—hundreds of them—come here everyday."

"So when you come here, like you are doing today, what do you expect to find?"

Gopal thought for a while, and said, "I'm looking to see if the holy man left me any message."

"How can he leave you a message when he is not here?"

Gopal got a little irritated by this question. "He's not like you and me," he responded, sharply. "He's the holy man. With him, anything is possible."

xxiv

No novel or movie ever captured the joy of a reunion so beautifully,—Gopal stood there beaming with gladness, while the holy man held out his arms in a show of aerial embrace.

"Did you miss me?" asked the holy man, as Gopal rushed into his arms to give him a hug.

"Yes,' replied Gopal. "A lot has happened since you went away. I was kidnapped, but I think you know about that already."

"Yes,—remember, I sent you a sign. What else is new?"

"There are some people who came to the hill that don't like you. I think they want to make trouble. I had to fight them."

"Did you win?" the holy man asked, bemusedly.

"Memsahib Linda and Raman held me back, or I would have thrashed all of them. They're no match for Gopal."

"Listen, when it comes to fighting, there are better ways to fight and win," said the holy man, weighing in with a piece of wisdom. "You will learn that as you grow older."

"I like the way I fight," protested Gopal.

"Of course…and how is school?"

"I like school very much," said Gopal, speaking to the holy man in English for the first time.

The holy man clapped his hands, showing admiration and pride. "Is arithmetic still your favorite subject?"

"Yes, I'm top of the class." Gopal was thoughtful for a moment, and then he said, "Maybe one day you'll teach me how to fight in that better way."

"I will," said the holy man. He looked at the boy as a father would at his son, full of tenderness and love. "Do you know, in my travels I heard that people are calling this place—our Mala Nagar—The Miracle of the Rose. Have you heard that?"

"No."

"Well, it's true."

"Tell me," said Gopal, "when you wander off, where do you go?"

"Places near and places far off,—places with names and places without names."

"There you go with your fancy talk," chided Gopal. "I guess it's part of being a holy man."

"You don't like my fancy talk?"

"No, I like you better when you talk normal."

"It's because you ask difficult questions. I don't get into a bus or a car to go traveling. Do you see what I mean?"

"No…but yes," said Gopal, resignedly. He had a lot of questions weighing on his mind,—about the homeless man, the rescue, the mysterious method by which the holy man managed to come and go as he pleased,—but he wasn't sure if these would be considered difficult questions. He decided to take a safer tack, and asked, "Well, now that you'r here, what are you going to do?"

"Do?...I didn't come here to do anything. I came here to rest and to meditate."

"That's just not possible, and you know it," said Gopal, in the manner of a teacher scolding a student for getting the answer completely wrong in a problem of logic. "Look at all the people outside, and most of them don't even know that you're back. Wait till you see the crowd tomorrow, and you'll change your mind."

"So, what do you propose I do?"

"I don't know."

The holy man reached for his duffel bag, searched inside, and pulled out a rose.

"I know what I'm going to do now. I want you to take this rose to the woman in the wheelchair who is with your memsahib. Then come back right away."

Gopal got the rose and flew out of the house. Linda and Raman were standing in the waiting area outside next to the peepul tree. Sushmita was talking to Asha, trying to keep her spirits up, while Bala was talking to an acquaintance he had met along the way.

"The holy man asked me to bring this to you," said Gopal, placing the rose on Asha's lap. He smiled at Linda, turned around, and ran back into the house.

Linda said to Raman, "I've never seen Gopal in such a hurry. I wonder what's going on inside."

Gopal's appearance and action took the people by surprise. If nothing else, it confirmed that the holy man was inside the house. More people joined in the singing of bhajans; and the beating of drums and the ringing of bells reached a crescendo.

Sushmita was ecstatic about the rose. Asha was feeling so badly that the import of the event bypassed her.

"I was saying she needed the holy man's blessing, and now she has it," said Sushmita, almost in tears. Asha held the rose close to her bosom, as Bala put his arm around her shoulder.

"Everything is going to be all right," he said to her, in a soothing voice, and Linda echoed that sentiment.

Some of the people in the crowd wanted to touch the rose, and Asha let them. One of these people was the man with the crutches.

"I'm going to stay here until I get to meet the holy man," he said, setting his crutches against the peepul tree and sitting down on the ground. "I'm not moving until I meet him."

Back inside the house, Gopal was ready for his next assignment, and was disappointed when the holy man told him there was nothing more to be done.

"What about the man with the crutches?" asked Gopal.

"What about him?"

"Well, shouldn't he get a rose also?"

"I'll think of something to give him tomorrow," said the holy man.

"How come you don't give a rose to memsahib?"

"She doesn't need one,—she's got you. And now, I'm going to sneak out of the house using the window in the back, like you used to do."

Gopal had a pensive look on his face. "How come you don't have to take a bus or a car to travel, but you have to sneak out by the window?"

"You're a smart boy," said the holy man, "and you do ask difficult questions. I want you to tell the people to continue singing and praying. And will you come back tomorrow morning with memsahib? I'll have some tasks for you."

"What time?"

"As early as you can make it. Tell me, do you sing or pray?"

"I don't like singing at all," said Gopal, and made a grimace as though he had tasted some unsavory food. "I don't think singing is for boys,—not boys who like to fight in battles. You don't hear about Emperor Akbar singing, do you?"

"No."

"What about praying?" insisted the holy man.

"Sometimes I've prayed to God to please make me the gilli danda champion of the world," admitted Gopal, meekly. He was used to doing all kinds of daring deeds in the face of adversity, and it shamed him slightly to admit that he had sought any help from God.

The holy man enjoyed watching various emotions play across the boy's face as he contemplated different topics. "Don't forget that one day you're going to be a famous architect, and you're going to build a palace right here. It will be called the *Palace of The Miracle of the Rose*."

This prospect did not thrill Gopal too much. He would abide by it, since the holy man put a large currency on it, but he did not see a lot of use for a palace unless you were a king and it was your residence.

As he was getting ready to leave, the holy man reached into his pocket and produced a coin that glittered like it was made of gold. He placed it in Gopal's hand.

"Keep this in a very safe place. In fact, give it to your memsahib to keep it safe for you. It's worth a lot of money."

Gopal studied the coin. It looked very old, and even though age had rubbed out most of the details, he could make out the picture of a king seated on a throne. Some of the details around the edges had also faded.

Gopal looked up to ask a question, but the holy man was no longer in the room.

XXV

The early morning arrival of Gopal the following day caused something of a stir, and people became charged with an urgency to get to the house because they felt that something important was going to happen.

Gopal was sitting on top of the world. He liked all the attention he was getting, especially those which came with small gifts. He was also the darling of the media because he alone was the conduit to the holy man, and he enjoyed his special status very much. What gave a significant lift to his buoyancy this morning, however, was the holy man's declaration that he was a rose to Memsahib Linda. "She doesn't need a rose because she has you," he had said. Those words wrapped their warmth around him and added a spring to his steps.

One-off vendors were also having a field day selling flower garlands, snacks, trinkets, and framed pictures of gods and goddesses. A chaiwallah had set up his cart on the side of the road, and had two portable charcoal stoves going simultaneously to satisfy the needs of a steady stream of customers.

The weather was agreeable, the temperature moderate, and a few clouds played hide-and-seek with the sun.

While Linda and Raman waited in line, Gopal skipped on ahead. When he got to the front of house, he was surrounded by members of the media right away.

"Did the holy man tell you yesterday what he has planned for today?" asked a reporter.

Gopal considered being inventive and making up a story, but foresaw the danger in it—he would lose face with the media if the event didn't come to pass. He noticed then that the man with the crutches was still there, sitting next to the peepul tree. Should he tell the reporter that the holy man planned to give him something? The question didn't nag him for long. He thought better of his impulse to share that tidbit, and said instead, "The holy man told me he was going to meditate for most of the day."

"Will you ask the holy man to come outside so we can take a few pictures?" asked a photographer, while he got Gopal and all the people crowding around him into the frame of his camera.

"I will," said Gopal, firmly. He knew that the photographers would want to include him in their pictures, and he rather liked the idea of being on the front pages again.

"Where's the lady you gave a rose to,—the lady in the wheelchair?" asked another reporter.

"She'll be coming here later," he said, for he wanted to appear knowledgeable.

"Is she still in the wheelchair?"

Gopal couldn't answer that question because he didn't know. He thought for a moment, and said, "It's not about the wheelchair,—it's about how she feels inside; and she's feeling pretty good."

Had the holy man been present for this exchange, he would have said that Gopal was a very clever boy.

The barrage of questions continued, as the crowd around Gopal grew. Seeing that the situation was getting a little out of hand, one of the policemen guarding the entrance to the house interceded and dispersed the crowd. Escorted by a policeman, Gopal made his way into the house.

"Hello, Gopal," said the holy man, smiling. "You're a regular celebrity…they can't get enough of you."

"You have to come outside so they can take a picture," said Gopal, cutting to the chase.

"What good will pictures do?"

"Well, newspaper stories have to have pictures. It makes them interesting."

"All right," said the holy man, "but I'm not going farther than the steps,—and only for a minute or two."

"And wear the dupatta," said Gopal. "It makes you look more like a holy man."

As soon as the holy man came out, the crowd surged forward. He offered the people a greeting of "namaste." The police immediately tightened security around the entrance. The chanting picked up tempo; drums and bells joined in. Gopal noticed that Linda and Raman were standing near the peepul tree and looking on.

"OK, we're going in now," whispered the holy man.

It was then that Gopal noticed the man on crutches struggling to move to the front of the crowd.

The holy man knew what Gopal was thinking.

"Go bring him to me. Ask the policeman to help you," he said.

The man on crutches was in a state of shock. He had wanted very badly to meet the holy man, but he couldn't believe that he was standing in front of him now, having been brought there by a police escort.

The holy man cupped his face with both hands.

"Give me your crutches," he said, in a soft voice.

The man obeyed.

The holy man got the crutches, held them up, and then flung them to the side, as a storm of flashbulbs went off.

A gasp went up among the crowd.

"You won't need them anymore," he said.

The man stood there unsure of himself, lost without his crutches. He took one small step forward, as a child might who is learning how to walk. With his hands stretched out in front of him for balance, his body more erect, he took another step. A soft smile broke on his face as he took a few more steps, still with some degree of caution. Once it dawned oh him that he was fully healed, tears of joy ran down his cheeks. He faced the house and prostrated himself, as a loud cheer went up among the crowd.

The holy man turned around and walked back into the house.

Once inside, the holy man said, "Now I have a task for you to perform. Are you familiar with the bicycle repair shop on Agni Street?"

"Yes, it's not far from my house," replied Gopal.

"There's a green shed right next to that shop, and there's a lost kitten that has taken refuge in the back of that shed. I want you to take that kitten and drop it off in the backyard of the house that is

sitting at the corner of Agni Street and Phalki Street. There, the kitten will meet its new owner,—
a girl who is feeling very lonely since her sister passed away."

"Should I talk to the people in the house?"

"Oh, there's no need for that," said the holy man.

"What about the woman in the wheelchair—Memsahib Linda's friend? What happened to her?
The reporters asked me about her."

"And what did you say?"

"I said she was feeling fine, but I didn't say anything about the wheelchair."

"Well, we've gotten rid of two things for two people," said the holy man. "The man won't be
needing his crutches, and your memsahib's friend won't be needing her wheelchair."

"And the kitten will have a new mistress!" exclaimed Gopal.

xxvi

Next day, it was back to school for Gopal. After the excitement of the previous two days, school
seemed rather dull. In maths class, they were learning addition and subtraction of fractions. In
English class,—where Gopal still lagged behind other students in his age group,—he was
learning the rudiments of the language using nursery rhymes. In science, gravity, laws of motion,
and friction took center stage.

Between bells, as students switched classes, the talk was all about Gopal. He had made the front
page of all the regional newspapers, and his classmates were eager to learn more details about all
the stories.

"It was *my* idea to help the man with the crutches," he boasted. "The holy man asked me what he
should do, and I told him that he should help the man who needed help the most. The holy man
always listens to my ideas."

Gopal was also a master of embellishments, and he transformed his simple actions into heroic
ones, making himself look like a superhero whom one encounters in swashbuckling movies and
comic books.

The history teacher started his class by giving Gopal five minutes of classtime to talk about his
escapades, so he could get it out of his system. The strategy didn't work too well because Gopal

wanted to go on and on once he stepped into the raconteur's shoes, and finally had to be told to sit down.

Recess saw Gopal at his best, as he added many new chapters to the weekend's story that rested on tenuous facts.

When school was over, Linda and Raman went directly to the tea stall, where Sushmita and Asha were waiting for them. The owner was happy to see them, because having Gopal there usually meant more business.

"I see you've added more tables," said Raman.

"Yesterday, I could have had 20 more tables, and it wouldn't have been enough."

Asha was looking chipper. She was a transformed woman, full of zest and animated conversation.

"I wish I had made it to the hill yesterday," she said, affecting a remorseful tone. "I would love to have seen the holy man fling those crutches!"

Just then, a uniformed man riding a bicycle stopped at their table, and handed a telegram to Linda. "I was on my way to the apartment, but since you are here…"

"I'm sure it's from Savitri," said Linda, accepting the envelope and tearing it open. "Yes, it is. She says she's arriving tomorrow by the evening express. She'll be a lot of fun to have around."

A strong breeze was blowing and it was playing with Linda'a golden tresses, tossing them around playfully. The way she brushed them back to their original symmetry belonged to the realm of poetry, thought Raman.

Raman's reverie was dislodged when the owner brought everyone chai and vada. "What's with the rescue of the kitten?" he asked. "Is there some special significance behind it?"

"If there's a message, it's that we should take care of the abandoned, lost, and helpless," chimed in Linda. "I think the holy man's focus was on the young girl who had lost her sister."

The miracles performed by the holy man made a wonderful topic of conversation, and everyone had plenty to say about them. Raman's attention, however, remained tangled up in contemplating Linda's beauty.

Gopal looked up from the food he was eating. Even though everyone was speaking in English, he had picked up on the gist of the conversation. "No one knows the holy man like I do," he said. "He came here to perform miracles, and he's not finished yet."

"What did the holy man tell you?" asked Sushmita.

"Nothing, but I know more miracles are going to happen,—that's why he's here."

"Gopal is such a tease," said Linda, giving him a friendly shove.

For the time being, it was good not to have the media surrounding them, and even though people at the adjoining tables were leaning in on their conversation, there was no interruption or intrusion to spoil the happy mood.

"I'm sad I didn't get to see the holy man, but I'm glad I got to see the miracle of the rose," said Sushmita. "I wish my husband could have been here as well, but someone has to take care of the business."

"Stay a few more days and you may get to see the holy man," said Linda. "And if Gopal is right, you'll have more miracles to witness."

"I am tempted," said Sushmita. "These are once-in-a-lifetime events. I'm sure my husband won't mind."

Linda happened to glance in Gopal's direction. She saw him sitting there, quite composed in the company of adults. He has grown a lot in these few weeks, she thought, and for a boy his age, he handles himself so well in challenging situations. "He's my little hero. I love him," she told herself.

She got up and walked over to his chair.

"Let's go for a little walk, you and I," she said.

Raman watched as Gopal stood up and took Linda's hand. Far removed from the clamor, drama, and excitement of the past few days, there was something domestic and endearing about the picture that was now in front of his eyes,—a tranquil picture of a woman and a child happy in their environment.

xxvii

Linda had been looking forward all day to seeing her friend. She reminisced with Raman about their Calcutta trip, and had many a laugh remembering the playfully combative way in which Savitri interacted with her husband. It was excellent theater and they had enjoyed it immensely. Savitri was also sharp with her opinions and had an incisive way of looking at things which made her an interesting conversationalist.

"I've brought you a little surprise," she said, getting off the train.

"Where's your luggage?" asked Linda, running forward to greet and embrace her friend.

"That's part of the surprise. I've brought someone along to carry the luggage for me."

"You don't mean…"

"Yes."

Just as she said this, Rishi stepped off the train carrying two pieces of luggage in his hands.

"What a surprise!" exclaimed Linda, as Raman and Rishi shook hands. "I'm glad Rishi was able to break away from work. The fun we're going to have is now doubled."

"I wouldn't say that for sure. He can be a stick-in-the-mud and a spoilsport," said Savitri, hoping to rub her husband the wrong way.

"I was hoping that you would get to enjoy my wife's company without me being in the picture, but that's not quite how it turned out," said Rishi, displaying his acerbic wit. "I'll try to keep a low profile."

"That's like Cleopatra saying she'll try not to look beautiful," came the quick repartee.

"We're glad you're both here," said Raman. "The hotels in Bijli offer better accommodation, but we've booked you at Hotel Sameer, knowing you'd want to be close to all the action."

On the taxi ride to the hotel, Linda and Raman brought their friends up-to-date with all the recent happenings.

"I can't wait to make my first visit to the hill," said Savitri, "but before that I've got to meet Gopal, and I've got to get to the tea stall,—the hub of all your activities."

"The owner would enjoy meeting you two," said Raman. "He's quite a character."

Savitri said that after checking in at the hotel and freshening up she'd be ready for any game, and Rishi added that, as a slave to her wishes and commands, he would follow suit.

They decided to meet at the tea stall at seven.

Quite often, heroes cut a smaller figure than the personas they project. Gopal, though, did not fit the mold of this generalization. Savitri had formed a mental picture of Gopal as someone brave, forward, and dashing, and the boy who stood in front of her, and shook her hand, fit that description to a T. She could easily picture him jumping into a room full of dacoits to rescue stolen jewels, or talking to a bunch of reporters with the aplomb of a politician.

"People are saying you are more popular than the movie stars," said Savitri.

"I plan to be in the movies," responded Gopal. "The holy man keeps talking about me becoming an architect and building a palace, but I think it's more fun to act in movies. But my first goal is to become the gilli danda champion of the world."

There were no customers at the tea stall waiting to order, so the owner joined them at the table.

"I was very skeptical of the holy man, but I've changed my mind about him. He has done a lot of good for this town; and he does have special powers,—there's no denying it."

"Why won't he talk to people?" asked Rishi. "What's your take on that?"

"I understand why he doesn't want to talk to people,—they can be very petty and disagreeable. After all, all the turbulence in the world is created by human beings. Give them something good and they'll find a way to muck it up in short order."

"Oh, come now," protested Rishi. "Surely there are a fair number of agreeable people in this world. You can't dismiss offhand all the people who have made great contributions to humanity."

"The great scientists, the great composers, the great story tellers, they're like the holy man, except that they operate in their secular fields. All greatness happens outside the rush of human beings, so there can be no mischief."

"I'm in your camp," said Savitri.

"Of course you are," returned Rishi. "If I'm on Camp North, you're on Camp South. That's how it goes,—that's why we are married."

"Oh, don't be so dramatic, dear," said Savitri, fanning her hands out in the air in a show of disappointment. "We're married because we fell in love…and we're still in love."

"If you say so."

"I was expecting a strong affirmation, not a whimpering concession," chided Savitri, playfully.

"Let's ask Gopal," said Raman, steering the conversation back to the original question, and proceeded to translate the problem for the boy.

Generally speaking, Gopal had a dim view of adult conversations. He thought they wasted a lot of time talking about trivial things, and this, as far as he was concerned, was just another fine example of it.

"When you're traveling all the time and performing miracles, you don't have time to be talking to people," he said, with the finality of a mathematician affixing a QED at the end of a theorem's proof. "When I become the gilli danda champion of the world, or when I become a famous architect, I won't have time to be talking to people either."

The conversation that followed touched on various topics—the heightened business at the tea stall, Rishi's work with the foundation, recent happenings in Calcutta, Raman's documentary, and Linda's academic work—and finally came to rest on the two recent miracles, which were on everyone's mind in Mala Nagar.

It had been arranged that Sushmita and Asha would go with them to the hill the next morning.

"Now that all members of the circle would be represented there," said Savitri, "I wonder if the holy man will put in an appearance."

"What do you think, Gopal?" asked Raman, giving him the gist of their conversation.

Gopal responded without any hesitation, and with cool nonchalance. "Of course he will."

xxviii

Gopal was wrong,—or to be fair, sort of wrong,—for when the "friends of the circle" got to the base of Praarthana Hill, they found the path ahead leading up to the house blocked by police.

Linda walked up to Sergeant Bedi, whose jeep was parked by the side of the road, and tried to get a read on the situation, but all he would say was that an investigation was under way that required a complete evacuation of the hill.

"You've never done anything like this before," said Linda. "Is it something serious?"

"I really cannot comment at this time," returned the sergeant. "I'll hold a press conference as soon as the matter is resolved." His demeanor was business-like, and Linda could tell that his mind was occupied with serious matters.

"Is the holy man still there?"

"Hard to tell. You know how it is,—his comings and goings are quite a mystery."

Not wanting to infringe on Sergeant Bedi's time, Linda withdrew and rejoined her friends.

Raman had just finished talking to some of the people about the goings-on during the past hour, and he discovered that police had brought boxes from the top of the hill and loaded them on to trucks.

"The house has nothing in it, so where are the boxes coming from?" asked Linda, mystified by the turn of events.

"And what could be in them?" asked Rishi.

"Bad luck," moaned Savitri. "Why did this have to happen now?"

"I can go to the house and find out," said Gopal, when he was apprised of the situation. "I'll ask the holy man,—he'll tell me."

Linda told him that the police wouldn't want him there in the middle of their investigation, to which Sushmita appended the comment that it might not be safe.

Anjali Dutt of the Daily Beacon was interviewing some people in the distance, and Raman and Rishi decided to join them to see if they could find out anything further.

The man she was talking to was none other than Rohit Kapadia, President of the PSUUR.

"Something fishy is going on in and around the house, that's for sure," declared the activist. "Mark my words, something smells very fishy."

"Will you tell us what you suspect is going on?" pressed the reporter.

"It's obvious, isn't it? The police don't come to your house or my house and haul away boxes of material."

"So what are you suggesting?"

"I'm not suggesting anything, for I don't have the facts. But mark my words,—when the news comes out, it's going to be ugly."

"Do you think all this has anything to do with the holy man?" asked Anjali.

"You can call him a holy man, but I won't. He's nothing but a fraudster," fulminated the activist.

Anjali noticed Raman and Rishi approaching her, and broke off the interview.

"Have you found out anything?" asked Raman.

"No. The police started their operation only after clearing the hill, so we have no eyewitness account. It's all conjecture right now. By the way, what do you think?"

"We heard about police removing boxes of material. Now that's a surprise. There's nothing in the house,—so what could they be removing?"

"The police are being very hush-hush about it," said Anjali. "Not a single comment, even off-the-record."

"We'll keep our ears to the ground," said Raman. "If we hear anything, we'll let you know."

The picture at the foot of the hill was very different today. The linearity and orderliness of the previous days had been replaced suddenly by pockets of agitated and uncertain activity, as though a sudden gust had blown through a placid field. People were trying to make sense of what was happening and what it meant.

Like everyone else, the "friends of the circle" were contemplating events of the day, when Linda noticed that Gopal was no longer in their midst.

"Where is Gopal? Where did he go to?" she asked, flustered by his absence.

"If I have to guess," said Savitri, "I bet he has snuck off to visit the holy man."

"I'm with you," said Rishi, in a rare moment of agreement. "He won't let uncertainty be his master."

"Do you think he will be able to get past police security?" asked Asha, who hadn't said anything so far. She was on the shy and retiring side,—just the opposite of Savitri, who was always gregarious and outspoken.

"I'm sure he will," said Raman, somewhat proudly. "Gopal is a master at war games."

"All we can do is wait and see," conceded Linda.

Since there wasn't anything that could be accomplished, they decided to walk to the tea stall, have a small breakfast, and wait for Gopal's return.

The owner of the tea stall had heard the news already from his other patrons. He was of the opinion that whatever it was that was engaging the police had nothing to do with the holy man or the house.

"What then?" asked Raman.

"Maybe it has something to do with the people who kidnapped Gopal,—that circle of gangsters. Remember, we still don't have any answers to that event."

xxix

Gopal moved cautiously, hiding behind tree trunks, boulders, and sometime lying down in the grass to avoid detection. A few people noticed him creeping up the side of the hill, but they didn't say anything to the police. They knew he was quite harmless, and he might bring them some news from the holy man.

It took Gopal nearly 20 minutes to get to the front of the house. The place looked very different, —gone was the crowd, the noise from the drums and the bells, and the singing of bhajans. He was expecting to find a swarm of policemen, but was surprised to discover only one stationed at the entrance. From here, the strategy was clear and simple: he would keep going up the hill, duck into the woods on the right, reverse direction, and then use the window in the back to sneak into the house.

Gopal wondered what the holy man thought of the difference in atmosphere surrounding the house. Maybe the lack of noise meant nothing to him. "I bet he travels with his mind to the riverbank whenever he wants complete peace," Gopal told himself. It was with these thoughts that Gopal reached the back of the house. He was about to step through the window when he heard a noise behind him in the distance. He turned around. Through the gaps in the trees, he saw two policemen. They were walking slowly and swatting the tall grass in front of them with their lathis as though they were looking for something. Gopal waited till their backs were turned to him and climbed through the window.

"Hello, Gopal," came the familiar voice, from the adjoining room. "I knew you would come."

"What's going on?" asked Gopal, cutting to the chase.

"I don't know,—you tell me."

"The police won't let anyone come up the hill to see you. Take a look outside,—there's no one here."

The holy man stepped out of the house with Gopal.

"It's very peaceful here," he said. "I like it this way."

"Why were the policemen carrying boxes with them? Did they get them from here?"

"How can they get them from here? There's nothing except for my duffel bad and my mat."

"I saw two policemen near the back of the house," informed Gopal. "They were a little distance away from me. They were searching the ground for something. I should go and take a look and see what they are up to."

"It's not important," said the holy man.

"It is to the people who want to come and see you," responded Gopal. "Memsahib has two friends visiting her from Calcutta. They were looking forward to coming here, and now they can't. Do you think the hill will be open to visitors tomorrow?"

"If I have to make a guess, I would say no."

"That's a rotten situation, especially when someone comes all the way from Calcutta." Never one to hide his feelings or emotions, Gopal gave free rein to his anger and frustration.

"We'll have to find a way around this problem then," said the holy man, in a calm and assuring voice. He took an envelope out of his duffel bag and gave it to Gopal, saying, "Give this to your memsahib."

Gopal took the holy man's response to mean that the problem would be solved, and declared his intention to snoop around behind the house.

"Don't get into any kind of trouble," said the holy man, as Gopal turned and headed towards the adjoining room.

Stepping out of the window, Gopal studied the surroundings and decided that they were free of police presence. He walked cautiously towards the spot where the two policemen had been conducting some sort of search. Finding nothing there, he went a little farther. About a hundred yards out, he found a spot where the grass had been disturbed to reveal a square piece of metal on the ground with a ring attached to it. A trap door, thought Gopal. He bent down, grabbed the ring, and pulled on it, but it was too heavy for him,—it would not give. Someone has opened it recently, he thought. It must be a storage space. Were there other storage spaces? Is that what the police were looking for? He was going to explore some more, but he heard a police whistle in the distance, and decided to backtrack. So, the things in the boxes were possibly coming from some storage spaces, and not from the house.

When Gopal got close to the house, he stopped again. There were two policemen now standing not far from the window. They were talking animately about something.

He hadn't had a decent conversation with the holy man, but he knew that he couldn't go back to the house. He decided to head back to town.

Gopal found going downhill more challenging than going uphill,—the surroundings opened out, and he felt more exposed. At anytime, he thought, some policeman was going to stop him and march him off in disgrace. However, that did not happen. He stayed away from the marked path and continued to climb down, so that when he got to the foot of the hill, he was not near any group of people.

He couldn't wait to share his discoveries with the group. Main Street offered the shortest distance to the tea stall, but he decided to take a series of side streets out of a sense of caution. Time and distance passed quickly as he mulled over all the things he had seen on the hill.

Linda was happy to see him. "What have you learned? Sit down and tell us," she said. "But make it snappy,—you've got to get to school. I brought your school bag and tiffin carrier."

Gopal liked telling long stories with a cornucopia of invented details decorating the facts,—the idea of brevity and succinctness was anathema to him. However, he had no choice in the matter, and provided a quick summary of the morning's escapade before being walked to school by Linda and Raman. It was just as he was saying bye that Gopal remembered that he had a note for Linda.

"Run along now," said Linda, accepting the note and giving him a hug.

"What an extraordinary morning," said Raman. "See what the note says."

The note was short and cryptic. It read:

The river has no barriers.
Om

"What do you make of that?" asked Linda.

"Beats me,—we'll ask the others when we get back to the tea stall."

Rishi was talking about Gopal's find when they rejoined the group.

"Seems to me that some illegal activity is going on," he said, in a hushed voice. "Question is who's involved and what is the nature of the activity."

"Why would anyone pick the hill for an illegal activity?" asked the owner, as he left the table to take care of a customer. "People are swarming all over the place, day and night."

"Look what we have," said Linda, sitting down. "A note from the holy man,—a very cryptic note."

"He has such beautiful handwriting," said Savitri, studying the note. "Of course, a river has no barrier, unless man builds a dam across it. So why is he stating the obvious?"

"That's the question," echoed Rishi.

"Of course it is, dear," said Savitri.

The owner rejoined them and picked up on the old thread. "I think whatever is in those underground spaces was hidden there before the holy man moved into the house. Otherwise it doesn't make any sense. I'm curious as to what the items are that the police are removing."

"Take a look at this," said Linda, handing the owner the note.

"What do you make of it? Why is he stating the obvious?" asked Savitri.

The owner was thoughtful for a moment. Then he said, "What *does* have a barrier is the hill. Why go to the hill which has a barrier, when you can go to the river which has no barrier. I think he is telling you to go to the river."

"Brilliant!" exclaimed Savitri. "How exciting to be right smack in the middle of a mystery. I think we should go to the river right now."

"We should give the holy man some time," suggested Rishi. "He just spoke to Gopal about an hour ago. He can't be at the riverbank right now."

"But, my dear, he's no ordinary man," explained Savitri.

xxx

Seven people set off from the tea stall to visit the riverbank. The group included the tea-stall owner, who had found someone to take care of his business while he was away.

"I feel like a member of an army marching toward a mission," said Savitri, quite excited by the prospect of what lay ahead.

"I'm keeping my expectations low," said Raman. "The holy man has never been seen anywhere except on the hill, and I can't see that picture changing."

Main Street was busy as usual with bicycles, scooters, carts, rickshaws, lorries, and an occasional bus, all moving towards their business destinations, bravely fighting congestion, while human beings moved in every possible direction like molecules in Brownian motion. Lying in the shade of a tree, two cows offered a contrasting picture of restfulness and contentment. Linda enjoyed taking an early-morning walk and feeling the energy of the town she had come to love. Some of the shopkeepers waved to her, and the owner of Laxman Sari Emporium, with whom she had exchanged some thoughts on Kanchipuram silk saris, walked with her a short distance, exchanging pleasantries.

"I love this time of the day," said Linda. "A brisk walk makes me feel right on top of the world."

"Can you believe this," said Sushmita, "my sister is walking with us as normal as normal can be, and just a few days ago she was having trouble just getting out of bed. I'm so happy for her."

Asha smiled.

People were not used to seeing the tea-stall owner walking in the streets without a business-purpose, and the fact that he was with Linda and five others provoked considerable curiosity, with the result that by the time they reached the riverbank, a satellite of people was attached to them.

"Why, there's no one here," said Savitri, looking around. A few boats and bamboo rafts were going down the river, and the gentle whisperings of the water and bird songs from the treetops filled the air.

"I stand by my reading of the message," said the tea-stall owner, noticing the disappointment on everyone's face. "The note had to have a purpose,—or else, why send it,—and the only meaning I could decipher was an invitation to visit the riverbank."

"Your reading was perfect," consoled Linda, and Raman concurred.

"We'll wait a little longer," added Savitri. "It's such a peaceful setting,—poetic, if you ask me,— we might as well enjoy it."

The satellite group of people didn't share the same outlook on the aesthetics of the location and decided to disperse.

"We've lost our little fan club," said Sushmita, as the receding figures grew smaller.

"I do wonder how long the police will have the hill locked down. I can spend two more days here but then I have to head back," said Rishi. "I have some very important meetings that I cannot afford to miss."

"Yes, he has to go back," added Savitri, "but I'll stay longer. I can't see the police taking more than a week with their operation."

Raman was about to say something but he stopped because he thought he heard some footsteps. Turning around, he saw someone walking towards the bench that was close to the bank.

"That looks like the homeless man," said Linda. "Could that be him? No one has seen him since the day that Gopal was kidnapped."

"A man can have no peace," complained the homeless man, when the group approached him. "No peace at all."

"Listen," said Raman, "we want to thank you for saving our boy. If it wasn't for you, who knows what might have happened."

"Oh, I was just passing by," said the homeless man, running his fingers through his scraggly beard. His face was dirty, and his legs were caked with mud.

"Where were you hiding?" asked Linda. "No one could find you. The police were looking for you, you know. So were all the newspaper reporters."

"I have no reason to hide from anybody," protested the homeless man. Then, looking with pleading eyes at all of them, he asked, "You wouldn't have some change to give to a hungry man, would you?"

Rishi produced a twenty rupee note from his pocket and gave it to him.

"Thank you,—thank you kindly, sahib! God will protect you. You're most generous."

"You haven't seen the holy man here by any chance, have you?" asked Rishi.

The homeless man ran his fingers over his forehead in a show of exasperation. "People are always asking me about the holy man. What do I know about him." He paused, and then added, "they do say he is in trouble."

"Who says he is in trouble?" asked Savitri.

"Why, some of the men on the boat this morning. They said the police raided the house on the hill and found smuggled goods. They said his holy-man stunt was just a front for a smuggling operation."

Linda was boiling over with rage. "That's all a bunch of lies!" she exploded. "The police didn't raid the house, and he's not running any smuggling operation. He's the most decent human being there is, a servant of God. How dare they say such unjust things about him!"

"It's sad that the world is full of lies," said the homeless man, "but there's also truth,—it hides in soft corners and puts on a show when the time is right."

"You're quite a philosopher," said the owner of the tea stall.

"No, no," protested the homeless man. "I just repeat some things I've heard in my wanderings. Living and sleeping outdoors, I get to hear a lot of things."

"What other profound things have you heard?" asked the owner.

"I've heard people say that faith is a tree with strong roots,—it cannot be shaken."

"Very true," agreed Sushmita. "After what the holy man did for my sister, we'll always believe in him."

Linda told the homeless man about the miracle that had restored Asha's health.

"I wish the holy man would perform a miracle and make my poverty go away," said the homeless man, with a laugh.

"You should go talk to the newspaper reporters about Gopal's rescue," said Savitri. "They'll give you some money for it."

"Oh, no, I was just kidding,—I'm quite wealthy being poor. I just need a few coins now and then to buy a meal or a cup of chai."

"You may come to my stall any time and I'll give you a free cup of chai," promised the owner.

"You are very kind."

Asha spoke for the first time. "I can bring you some clothes if you will come back here tomorrow. I have a lot of clothes that don't fit my husband since he has put on weight. I think they'll fit you."

"Don't trouble yourself, but I thank you. You all are very kind. May God bless you. I also make a little bit of money on the side making paper flowers, which sees me through some rough patches."

He then took a dirty, folded piece of paper from his pocket, and very quickly and deftly shaped it into a flower with a stem.

"For you," he said, giving it to Linda. "And now I must go. My friend will be coming by with his boat to give me a ride to the other side. The Hanuman temple is feeding the homeless. I never miss any of their meals,—their payasam is divine."

With that he walked away and soon was lost from sight.

Linda looked at the paper flower in her hand. It had been hastily put together and was starting to become unfurled near the stem. She wished she had a piece of tape to keep the folds together. It was then she noticed that there was some writing on the paper. The handwriting looked familiar. She undid the folds and stretched out the paper. In the middle of the dirty paper were these words:

The river has no barrier.

The End

Other Books by Ramnath Subramanian

The House on Prayer Hill (a novel)
ISBN 978-1387695188

After suffering two divorces and realizing that she was a poor judge of men, Linda Stevens decides to pursue a degree in anthropology. The research project she selects,—Pottery and Image Makers of India,—lands her in the town of Mala Nagar, where a holy man and a 10-year-old boy named Gopal enter the circle of her life. The holy man who has taken residence in a burned-out house on Prayer Hill, performs two miracles,—almost reluctantly,—that put the town on the regional map. Linda also befriends the filmmaker Venkat Raman, who decides to produce a documentary about the happenings on Prayer Hill. The holy man talks to Gopal and no one else, and has him participate in the miracles, which make the young boy everyone's darling in town. While capturing the special bond that exists between the holy man and Gopal, and between "Memsahib" Linda and Gopal, the story offers a window into the charms of Indian life, and points to the profound depths of religion and philosophy that underscore it. This is the first in a trilogy of novels.

Zeek the Photographer (a novel)
ISBN 978-1716253881

Susan Murphy cannot walk away from her failed marriage because the memory of her husband, Zeek, saving her from a burning building keeps getting in the way. Instead, she puts in for a job transfer and gets assigned to the Madolina retail chain store in Florence, Italy. There she meets Antonio Corelli and finds new beginnings. Meanwhile, Zeek quits his teaching job and takes up photography as a profession, encouraged and inspired by Bridgit Muller, whom he meets by happenstance while taking a walk along the Rhine. Bridgit's rise to stardom as Zeek's model is a story of love, betrayal, and growth, set mostly in Rome, Florence, Venice, and London.

Bridgit the Model (a novel)
ISBN 978-1008942974

After suffering an unexpected betrayal by her photographer companion and lover, the media-savvy and much celebrated model, Bridgit, whose sensuous poses are displayed on billboards all across Europe, attempts to put her life back together. Chance encounters with a lost dog and a boy whom she befriended in an alley in Rome, act as catalysts for the "Mona Lisa of Advertising" to embark on a new path, while still pursuing fame. The story set sumptuously in Rome and Florence, filled with literary and artistic allusions, and powered by love, is one of transformation, transcendence, and triumph.

A Touch Of Miracle (a novella)

ISBN 978-1105032745

Sanjay, an orphan, who is living in Calcutta with his grandmother, has dropped out of college to write a novel. The temple town of Guruvayoor is the setting for his novel, and in the story it becomes a sanctuary for a young girl named Rani who has run away from home to avoid an unwanted marriage. A series of miracles at the temple reorient Rani's life and strengthen her faith. As Sanjay is penning a story filled with miracles, he cannot account for some of the chapters he has written. Even though they are in his handwriting, he cannot remember ever writing them. His friend, Radhika, helps him in his literary pursuit and offers moral support. Together they tackle the mystery surrounding them and become the beneficiaries of small miracles themselves.

A Second Meeting (a novella)

ISBN 978-1312447462

Kenneth, a successful businessman, whose wife died 19 years ago when she was just 23 years old, lives with memories of her, holding on to the philosophy that in one lifetime you can truly and fully love only one person. But what if life and death have dimensions and realities that are beyond our understanding? A series of discoveries, — many of them involving Susanna, a recently hired kitchen help who happens to be a prodigy with the piano—force Kenneth to rethink his philosophy and to reorient his life. While serendipity and happenstance play their hand, Amira, a piano coach to Susanna, seems to have the measure of the mysteries that are swirling around in the household.

A Sprinkling Of Pixie Dust: Essays on Education and Classroom Practices

ISBN 978-1716116117

What lessons do green-haired boys teach us? What misadventures happen when a teacher allows his students to chase an invisible rabbit in search of a story? Can you have a boredom factor of 4, and still be successful in school? Is the crown on the king's head what the spider saw? These and other ideas are explored in this collection of essays culled from my newspaper columns published in the El Paso Times between 1998 and 2019.

Arrow and A Song: Essays on Language, Fine Arts, and Travel

ISBN 978-1716266539

Language should march with vigor and move like a minuet. Great art can melt away the world, and a great symphony can make the world stand still. Travel can take one to serendipity's stations. These and other ideas are explored in this collection of essays culled from my newspaper columns published in the El Paso Times between 1998 and 2019.

Feathers 1,2,3: Essays on Nature and Animals
ISBN 978-1716231384

Welcome to the pyramid of the rose, the Danube of the wisteria, the towering peak of the ocotillo. Welcome, also, to the Taj Mahal of the peacock, the royal barge of the grackle, and the temple of the caparisoned elephant. These and other delectations from nature are explored in this collection of essays culled from my newspaper columns published in the El Paso Times between 1998 and 2019.

A Melody Of Flying Flutes: Essays On People, Places, And Things, Remembered
ISBN 978-1716199240

I am happy when I see atoms dance. I like the conversation of strangers in new places. I like turning the pages of books, and going on new journeys to new places. I like to hear the whistle of a train leaving a platform, nudging the compass needle to a new resting place. I like the sound of a ship's horn announcing a departure to a new destination. The sun shines with vigor. The river sings joyously. All is gold and blessed. These and other ideas are explored in this collection of essays culled from my newspaper columns published in the El Paso Times between 1998 and 2019.

The Message In The Rain: An otherworldly love story
ISBN 978-1716064807

A bereaved husband chases after the memories of his wife in a war-torn country, and receives signs and messages that point to a reunion on the 'other side.' Ian's path intersects with those of a few people — enigmas themselves — who help to shed light on the mysteries embedded in the messages.

Prisms and Bells: A collection of poems
ISBN 978-1716185922

The knowledge of the sun that is young once only inspires us to bring wings and passion to all the things we wish to accomplish in life. At the heart of poetry is a desire to make language sing a different song than has been heard before. When and where it succeeds, poetry offers a new country on the map that is full of delectations.

The Bridge to Bridgit
ISBN 978-1387924219

Famed and celebrated European model, Bridgit Muller, dubbed the Mona Lisa of Advertising, has set forth in this book her thoughts on a wide variety of subjects. Combining graceful language and a poetic idiom, these colorful and robust excursions into the realm of personal truths reveal a sensitive soul that is keenly aware that life is more than billboards and magazine covers splashed with sensuous poses. People who read this book — especially those who are familiar with Bridgit's triumphs in the fashion world — will be amazed at the depth and perspicacity she brings to the commonplace and complex aspects of the world at large.

Sticky Wicket and Other Vexations
ISBN 978-1387924219

Brian Cleary was among a handful of workers who still wore a purple tie to work. He eschewed the red tie, as he did the Brain Tonic which was reputed to increase productivity at work, because he was suspicious about both of them. But how long can he abide the pressures building up around him to conform to his milieu? What will he do and how will things turn out? There are other vexations in the world that are real rather than fictional, and I had addressed them in several of my weekly newspaper columns published in the El Paso Times between 1998 and 2019. Here, the dystopian story and a selection of my newspaper columns set up a sticky wicket for our times, and offer a panoply of ideas for reflections and resolution.

The Bus To Agra (a novel)
ISBN: 978-1716140785

After finding out that her fiancé has been cheating on her, Jennifer Blaise runs away to India to seek a new direction in her life. On her flight to New Delhi, she meets widower, Kiran Patel, who invites her to stay with his family in Nana Nagar until she is able to find proper accommodations. Jennifer becomes fast friends with Kiran's daughter-in-law, Radha, and is drawn to a homeless boy named Nanda. When she tries to enroll Nanda in school, she meets an independent journalist, Jai Jaiprakash, who becomes an important part of her life. Jai is shy when it comes to matters of the heart, and Jennifer has tossed romance aside after being jilted in love. Will the bus trip to Agra change things? What role will Nanda's "mandir" rock, which he gives to Jennifer as a talisman, play in the outcome of events? Life in India—-with all its eccentricities, charms, and wisdom—comes to life in this endearing West-meets-East love story.

The Sariwallah (a novel)
ISBN: 978-1458390424

Rachel Flynn came to India to gather material for her second novel. She settled happily in a charming town full of friendly people, -that is, until the anonymous notes started to arrive. "If you know what's good for you, you'll stay away from the American woman. If you don't heed this warning, things will get very nasty for you," warned the first note, sent to a school master who had brought Rachel as a guest speaker to his classroom. As Police Chief Motilal proceeds with his investigation and starts connecting the dots, he discovers that there's more to the notes than meets the eye. Who is writing the notes? What is the hidden motive behind them? Will Motilal uncover the plot before something serious happens? Along the way as the story unfolds, the reader is treated to some colorful characters and the infinite charms of Indian life.

Journey To A Second Spring (a novel)
ISBN: 978-1435780477

For five years, Jake Johns made a living playing the stock market. He then started to dabble in craps at a Las Vegas casino, because he found comfort in mathematics and a sureness in numbers- elements which were missing in his 12-year marriage. During one of his gaming sessions at Drake's Diamond Casino, he encounters Holly Simmons, who makes big bets and has a unique and reckless way of throwing the dice. Attracted to the "heretic shooter," first by her play and then by the obtuseness of her personality, he manages to forge a friendship which makes him reevaluate his marriage and his life's goals. Will he come out richer or poorer, smarter or foolish, from his new dalliance with gambling and a mystery woman? Holly soon becomes a Las Vegas celebrity because of her shooting style and the enormous success she enjoys at the craps table. She shoots with her eyes closed, and is often seen talking to herself before throwing the dice. People are convinced that there is an outside force that is guiding her hand. Who is Holly, the reclusive resident at the casino's hotel, and what is the story of her life? Craps aficionados will enjoy this story as much as romantics, who believe in the eternal and otherworldly aspects of true love.

The Flower Girl of Panipat (a novel)
ISBN: 978-1387873449

Two crossword clues had something to do with Jim Driscoll going to Panipat, India, to be a resident at the Neela Akash Writers' Retreat. Once there, a flower girl— who first appeared to him in a dream, and then in real life (are they the same person?)—takes him on a journey of serendipitous discoveries. While staying at the retreat, widower Jim is drawn to the charms of Indian author Kamala Sharma, whose singsong voice makes him a prisoner so as to make the world disappear outside her circumference. Both are fascinated by the identity of the flower girl and the mysterious way in which she injects herself into Jim's life. In her final manifestation, the flower girl performs a miracle that changes the lives of Jim and Kamala forever. The story captures the delightfulness and appeal of Indian life, while at the same time pointing to the profound depths of religion and philosophy that inform and underscore it.

Talkative Man Talks…and other conversations
ISBN: 978-1387810826

During the course of writing a weekly newspaper column for the El Paso Times for 20 years, I invented several characters—Talkative Man, The Whip, the Mayor of Trance Town, among them —whose conversations and interactions provided a useful vehicle for carrying certain ideas forward. I took this approach in the belief that satirical, verbal exchanges between colorful characters in whimsical settings—such as, the Loose Marbles School District—can expose the cracks in human nature and political systems with greater economy and alacrity than regular prose. In the vignettes included in this collection, a removal of the disguise of nonsense and flamboyancy offers a window through which the real world comes into view, replete with contradictions, corruptions, and celebrations.

Lightning Source UK Ltd.
Milton Keynes UK
UKHW050645211122
412554UK00015B/724